THE
WAYS OF MEN

ELIOT GREGORY

1st WORLD
LIBRARY
Literary Society

The Ways of Men

Eliot Gregory

© 1st World Library – Literary Society, 2004
PO Box 2211
Fairfield, IA 52556
www.1stworldlibrary.org
First Edition

LCCN: 2005901314

Softcover ISBN: 1-4218-1129-4
Hardcover ISBN: 1-4218-1029-8
eBook ISBN: 1-4218-1229-0

Purchase *"The Ways of Men"*
as a traditional bound book at:
www.1stWorldLibrary.org/purchase.asp?ISBN=1-4218-1129-4

1st World Library Literary Society is a nonprofit organization dedicated to promoting literacy by:

- Creating a free internet library accessible from any computer worldwide.
- Hosting writing competitions and offering book publishing scholarships.

The Ways of Men
contributed by Tim, Ed & Rodney
in support of
1st World Library Literary Society

CHAPTER 1

"UNCLE SAM"

The gentleman who graced the gubernatorial armchair of our state when this century was born happened to be an admirer of classic lore and the sonorous names of antiquity.

It is owing to his weakness in bestowing pompous cognomens on our embryo towns and villages that to-day names like Utica, Syracuse, and Ithaca, instead of evoking visions of historic pomp and circumstance, raise in the minds of most Americans the picture of cocky little cities, rich only in trolley-cars and Methodist meeting-houses.

When, however, this cultured governor, in his ardor, christened one of the cities Troy, and the hill in its vicinity Mount Ida, he little dreamed that a youth was living on its slopes whose name was destined to become a household word the world over, as the synonym for the proudest and wealthiest republic yet known to history, a sobriquet that would be familiar in the mouths of races to whose continents even the titles of Jupiter or Mars had never penetrated.

A little before this century began, two boys with packs bound on their stalwart shoulders walked from New

York and established a brickyard in the neighborhood of what is now Perry Street, Troy. Ebenezer and Samuel Wilson soon became esteemed citizens of the infant city, their kindliness and benevolence winning for them the affection and respect of the community.

The younger brother, Samuel, was an especial favorite with the children of the place, whose explorations into his deep pockets were generally rewarded by the discovery of some simple "sweet" or home-made toy. The slender youth with the "nutcracker" face proving to be the merriest of playfellows, in their love his little band of admirers gave him the pet name of "Uncle Sam," by which he quickly became known, to the exclusion of his real name. This is the kindly and humble origin of a title the mere speaking of which to-day quickens the pulse and moistens the eyes of millions of Americans with the same thrill that the dear old flag arouses when we catch sight of it, especially an unexpected glimpse in some foreign land.

With increasing wealth the brickyard of the Wilson brothers was replaced by an extensive slaughtering business, in which more than a hundred men were soon employed - a vast establishment for that day, killing weekly some thousand head of cattle. During the military operations of 1812 the brothers signed a contract to furnish the troops at Greenbush with meat, "packed in full bound barrels of white oak"; soon after, Samuel was appointed Inspector of Provisions for the army.

It is a curious coincidence that England also should have taken an ex-army-contractor as her patron saint, for if we are to believe tradition, St. George of Cappadocia filled that position unsatisfactorily before he passed through martyrdom to sainthood.

True prototype of the nation that was later to adopt him as its godfather, the shrewd and honest patriot, "Uncle Sam," not only lived loyally up to his contracts, giving full measure and of his best, but proved himself incorruptible, making it his business to see that others too fulfilled their engagements both in the letter and the spirit; so that the "U.S." (abbreviation of United States) which he pencilled on all provisions that had passed his inspection became in the eyes of officers and soldiers a guarantee of excellence. Samuel's old friends, the boys of Troy (now enlisted in the army), naively imagining that the mystic initials were an allusion to the pet name they had given him years before, would accept no meats but "Uncle Sam's," murmuring if other viands were offered them. Their comrades without inquiry followed this example; until so strong did the prejudice for food marked "U.S." become, that other contractors, in order that their provisions should find favor with the soldiers, took to announcing "Uncle Sam" brands.

To the greater part of the troops, ignorant (as are most Americans to-day) of the real origin of this pseudonym, "Uncle Sam's" beef and bread meant merely government provisions, and the step from national belongings to an impersonation of our country by an ideal "Uncle Sam" was but a logical sequence.

In his vigorous old age, Samuel Wilson again lived on Mount Ida, near the estates of the Warren family, where as children we were taken to visit his house and hear anecdotes of the aged patriot's hospitality and humor. The honor in which he was held by the country-side, the influence for good he exerted, and the informal tribunal he held, to which his neighbors came to get their differences straightened out by his common sense, are still talked of by the older inhabitants. One story in particular used to charm our boyish ears. It was about a dispute over land between the Livingstons and the Van Rensselaers, which was brought to an end by "Uncle Sam's" producing a barrel of old papers (confided to him by both families during the war, for safe keeping) and extracting from this original "strong box" title deeds to the property in litigation.

Now, in these troubled times of ours, when rumors of war are again in the air, one's thoughts revert with pleasure to the half-mythical figure on the threshold of the century, and to legends of the clear-eyed giant, with the quizzical smile and the tender, loyal heart, whose life's work makes him a more lovable model and a nobler example to hold up before the youth of to-day than all the mythological deities that ever disported themselves on the original Mount Ida.

There is a singular fitness in this choice of "Uncle Sam" as our patron saint, for to be honest and loyal and modest, to love little children, to do one's duty quietly in the heyday of life, and become a mediator in old age, is to fulfil about the whole duty of man; and every patriotic heart must wish the analogy may be long maintained, that our loved country, like its prototype, may continue the protector of the feeble and a peace-maker among nations.

CHAPTER 2

DOMESTIC DESPOTS

Those who walk through the well-to-do quarters of our city, and glance, perhaps a little enviously as they pass, toward the cheerful firesides, do not reflect that in almost every one of these apparently happy homes a pitiless tyrant reigns, a misshapen monster without bowels of compassion or thought beyond its own greedy appetites, who sits like Sinbad's awful burden on the necks of tender women and distracted men. Sometimes this incubus takes the form of a pug, sometimes of a poodle, or simply a bastard cur admitted to the family bosom in a moment of unreflecting pity; size and pedigree are of no importance; the result is always the same. Once Caliban is installed in his stronghold, peace and independence desert that roof.

We read daily of fathers tyrannizing over trembling families, of stepmothers and unnatural children turning what might be happy homes into amateur Infernos, and sigh, as we think of martyrdoms endured by overworked animals.

It is cheering to know that societies have been formed for the protection of dumb brutes and helpless children. Will no attempt be made to alleviate this other form of suffering, which has apparently escaped the eye of the reformer?

The animal kingdom is divided - like all Gaul - into three divisions: wild beasts, that are obliged to hustle for themselves; laboring and producing animals, for which man provides because they are useful to him - and dogs! Of all created things on our globe the canine race have the softest "snap." The more one thinks about this curious exception in their favor the more unaccountable it appears. We neglect such wild things as we do not slaughter, and exact toil from domesticated animals in return for their keep. Dogs alone, shirking all cares and labor, live in idle comfort at man's expense.

When that painful family jar broke up the little garden party in Eden and forced our first parents to work or hunt for a living, the original Dog (equally disgusted with either alternative) hit on the luminous idea of posing as the champion of the disgraced couple, and attached himself to Adam and Eve; not that he approved of their conduct, but simply because he foresaw that if he made himself companionable and cosy he would be asked to stay to dinner.

From that day to the present, with the exception of occasionally watching sheep and houses - a lazy occupation at the best - and a little light carting in Belgium (dogs were given up as turn-spits centuries ago, because they performed that duty badly), no canine has raised a paw to do an honest day's work, neither has any member of the genus been known voluntarily to perform a useful act.

How then - one asks one's self in a wonder - did the myth originate that Dog was the friend of Man? Like a multitude of other fallacies taught to innocent children, his folly must be unlearned later. Friend of man, indeed! Why, the "Little Brothers of the Rich" are guileless philanthropists in comparison with most canines, and unworthy to be named in the same breath with them. Dogs discovered centuries ago that to live in luxury, it was only necessary to assume an exaggerated affection for some wealthy mortal, and have since proved themselves past masters in a difficult art in which few men succeed. The number of human beings who manage to live on their friends is small, whereas the veriest mongrel cur contrives to enjoy food and lodging at some dupe's expense.

Facts such as these, however, have not over-thrown the great dog myth. One can hardly open a child's book without coming across some tale of canine intelligence and devotion. My tender youth was saddened by the story of one disinterested dog that refused to leave his master's grave and was found frozen at his post on a bleak winter's morning. With the experience of years in pet dogs I now suspect that, instead of acting in this theatrical fashion, that pup trotted home from the funeral with the most prosperous and simple-minded couple in the neighborhood, and after a substantial meal went to sleep by the fire. He must have been a clever dog to get so much free advertisement, so probably strolled out to his master's grave the next noon, when people were about to hear him, and howled a little to keep up appearances.

I have written "the richest and most simple minded couple," because centuries of self-seeking have developed in these beasts an especial aptitude for spotting possible victims at a glance. You will rarely find dogs coquetting with the strong-minded or wasting blandishments where there is not the probability of immediate profit; but once let even a puppy get a tenderhearted girl or aged couple under his influence, no pity will be shown the victims.

There is a house not a square away from Mr. Gerry's philanthropic headquarters, where a state of things exists calculated to extract tears from a custom-house official. Two elderly virgins are there held in bondage by a Minotaur no bigger than your two fists. These good dames have a taste for travelling, but change of climate disagrees with their tyrant. They dislike house-keeping and, like good Americans, would prefer hotel life, nevertheless they keep up an establishment in a cheerless side street, with a retinue of servants, because, forsooth, their satrap exacts a back yard where he can walk of a morning. These spinsters, although loving sisters, no longer go about together, Caligula's nerves being so shaken that solitude upsets them. He would sooner expire than be left alone with the servant, for the excellent reason that his bad temper and absurd airs have made him dangerous enemies below stairs - and he knows it!

Another household in this city revolves around two brainless, goggle-eyed beasts, imported at much expense from the slopes of Fuji-yama. The care that is lavished on those heathen monsters passes belief. Maids are employed to carry them up and down stairs, and men are called in the night to hurry for a doctor when Chi has over-eaten or Fu develops colic; yet their devoted mistress tells me, with tears in her eyes, that in spite of this care, when she takes her darlings for a walk they do not know her from the first stranger that passes, and will follow any boy who whistles to them in the street.

What revolts me in the character of dogs is that, not content with escaping from the responsibilities entailed on all the other inhabitants of our globe by the struggle for existence, these four-legged Pecksniffs have succeeded in making for themselves a fallacious reputation for honesty and devotion. What little lingering belief I had in canine fidelity succumbed then I was told that St. Bernards - those models of integrity and courage - have fallen into the habit of carrying the flasks of brandy that the kind monks provide for the succor of snowbound travellers, to the neighboring hamlets and exchanging the contents for - chops!

Will the world ever wake to the true character of these four-legged impostors and realize that instead of being disinterested and sincere, most family pets are consummate hypocrites. Innocent? Pshaw! Their pretty, coaxing ways and pretences of affection are unadulterated guile; their ostentatious devotion, simply a clever manoeuvre to excite interest and obtain unmerited praise. It is useless, however, to hope that things will change. So long as this giddy old world goes on waltzing in space, so long shall we continue to be duped by shams and pin our faith on frauds, confounding an attractive bearing with a sweet disposition and mistaking dishevelled hair and eccentric appearance for brains. Even in the Orient, where dogs have been granted immunity from other labor on the condition that they organized an effective street-cleaning department, they have been false to their trust and have evaded their contracts quite as if they were Tammany braves, like whom they pass their days in slumber and their nights in settling private disputes, while the city remains uncleaned.

I nurse yet another grudge against the canine race!

That Voltaire of a whelp, who imposed himself upon our confiding first parents, must have had an important pull at headquarters, for he certainly succeeded in getting the decree concerning beauty and fitness which applies to all mammals, including man himself, reversed in favor of dogs, and handed down to his descendants the secret of making defects and deformities pass current as qualities. While other animals are valued for sleek coats and slender proportions, canine monstrosities have always been in demand. We do not admire squints or protruding under jaws in our own race, yet bulldogs have persuaded many weak-minded people that these defects are charming when combined in an individual of their breed.

The fox in the fable, who after losing his tail tried to make that bereavement the fashion, failed in his undertaking; Dutch canal-boat dogs have, however, been successful where the fox failed, and are to-day pampered and prized for a curtailment that would condemn any other animal (except perhaps a Manx cat) to a watery grave at birth.

I can only recall two instances where canine sycophants got their deserts; the first tale (probably apocryphal) is about a donkey, for years the silent victim of a little terrier who had been trained to lead him to water and back. The dog - as might have been expected - abused the situation, while pretending to be very kind to his charge, never allowed him to roll on the grass, as he would have liked, or drink in peace, and harassed the poor beast in many other ways, getting, however, much credit from the neighbors for devotion and intelligence. Finally, one day after months of waiting, the patient victim's chance came. Getting his tormentor well out into deep water, the donkey quietly sat down on him.

The other tale is true, for I knew the lady who provided in her will that her entire establishment should be kept up for the comfort and during the life of the three fat spaniels that had solaced her declining years. The heirs tried to break the will and failed; the delighted domestics, seeing before them a period of repose, proceeded (headed by the portly housekeeper) to consult a "vet" as to how the life of the precious legatees might be prolonged to the utmost. His advice was to stop all sweets and rich food and give each of the animals at least three hours of hard exercise a day. From that moment the lazy brutes led a dog's life. Water and the detested "Spratt" biscuit, scorned in happier days, formed their meagre ordinary; instead of somnolent airings in a softly cushioned landau they were torn from chimney corner musings to be raced through cold, muddy streets by a groom on horseback.

Those two tales give me the keenest pleasure. When I am received on entering a friend's room with a chorus of yelps and attacked in dark corners by snarling little hypocrites who fawn on me in their master's presence, I humbly pray that some such Nemesis may be in store for these faux bonhommes before they leave this world, as apparently no provision has been made for their punishment in the next.

CHAPTER 3

CYRANO, ROSTAND, COQUELIN

Among the proverbs of Spanish folk-lore there is a saying that good wine retains its flavor in spite of rude bottles and cracked cups. The success of M. Rostand's brilliant drama, Cyrano de Bergerac, in its English dress proves once more the truth of this adage. The fun and pathos, the wit and satire, of the original pierce through the halting, feeble translation like light through a ragged curtain, dazzling the spectators and setting their enthusiasm ablaze.

Those who love the theatre at its best, when it appeals to our finer instincts and moves us to healthy laughter and tears, owe a debt of gratitude to Richard Mansfield for his courage in giving us, as far as the difference of language and rhythm would allow, this chef d'oeuvre unchanged, free from the mutilations of the adapter, with the author's wishes and the stage decorations followed into the smallest detail. In this way we profit by the vast labor and study which Rostand and Coquelin gave to the original production.

Rumors of the success attained by this play in Paris soon floated across to us. The two or three French booksellers here could not import the piece fast enough to meet the ever increasing demand of our reading public. By the time spring came, there were few cultivated people who had not read the new work and discussed its original language and daring treatment.

On arriving in Paris, my first evening was passed at the Porte St. Martin. After the piece was over, I dropped into Coquelin's dressing-room to shake this old acquaintance by the hand and give him news of his many friends in America.

Coquelin in his dressing-room is one of the most delightful of mortals. The effort of playing sets his blood in motion and his wit sparkling. He seemed as fresh and gay that evening as though there were not five killing acts behind him and the fatigue of a two-hundred-night run, uninterrupted even by Sundays, added to his "record."

After the operation of removing his historic nose had been performed and the actor had resumed his own clothes and features, we got into his carriage and were driven to his apartment in the Place de l'Etoile, a cosy museum full of comfortable chairs and priceless bric-a-brac. The conversation naturally turned during supper on the piece and this new author who had sprung in a night from obscurity to a globe-embracing fame. How, I asked, did you come across the play, and what decided you to produce it?

Coquelin's reply was so interesting that it will be better to repeat the actor's own words as he told his tale over the dismantled table in the tranquil midnight hours.

"I had, like most Parisians, known Rostand for some time as the author of a few graceful verses and a play (Les Romanesques) which passed almost unnoticed at the Francais.

"About four years ago Sarah Bernhardt asked me to her 'hotel' to hear M. Rostand read a play he had just completed for her. I accepted reluctantly, as at that moment we were busy at the theatre. I also doubted if there could be much in the new play to interest me. It was La Princesse Lointaine. I shall remember that afternoon as long as I live! From the first line my attention was riveted and my senses were charmed. What struck me as even more remarkable than the piece was the masterly power and finish with which the boyish author delivered his lines. Where, I asked myself, had he learned that difficult art? The great actress, always quick to respond to the voice of art, accepted the play then and there.

"After the reading was over I walked home with M. Rostand, and had a long talk with him about his work and ambitions. When we parted at his door, I said: 'In my opinion, you are destined to become the greatest dramatic poet of the age; I bind myself here and now to take any play you write (in which there is a part for me) without reading it, to cancel any engagements I may have on hand, and produce your piece with the least possible delay.' An offer I don't imagine many young poets have ever received, and which I certainly never before made to any author.

"About six weeks later my new acquaintance dropped in one morning to read me the sketch he had worked out for a drama, the title role of which he thought would please me. I was delighted with the idea, and told him to go ahead. A month later we met in the street. On asking him how the play was progressing, to my astonishment he answered that he had abandoned that idea and hit upon something entirely different. Chance had thrown in his way an old volume of Cyrano de Bergerac's poems, which so delighted him that he had been reading up the life and death of that unfortunate poet. From this reading had sprung the idea of making Cyrano the central figure of a drama laid in the city of Richelieu, d'Artagnan, and the Precieuses Ridicules, a seventeenth-century Paris of love and duelling.

"At first this idea struck me as unfortunate. The elder Dumas had worked that vein so well and so completely, I doubted if any literary gold remained for another author. It seemed foolhardy to resuscitate the Three Guardsmen epoch - and I doubted if it were possible to carry out his idea and play an intense and pathetic role disguised with a burlesque nose.

"This contrasting of the grotesque and the sentimental was of course not new. Victor Hugo had broken away from classic tradition when he made a hunchback the hero of a drama. There remained, however, the risk of our Parisian public not accepting the new situation seriously. It seemed to me like bringing the sublime perilously near the ridiculous.

"Fortunately, Rostand did not share this opinion or my doubts. He was full of enthusiasm for his piece and confident of its success. We sat where we had met, under the trees of the Champs Elysees, for a couple of hours, turning the subject about and looking at the question from every point of view. Before we parted the poet had convinced me. The role, as he conceived it, was certainly original, and therefore tempting, opening vast possibilities before my dazzled eyes.

"I found out later that Rostand had gone straight home after that conversation and worked for nearly twenty hours without leaving the study, where his wife found him at daybreak, fast asleep with his head on a pile of manuscript. He was at my rooms the next day before I was up, sitting on the side of my bed, reading the result of his labor. As the story unfolded itself I was more and more delighted. His idea of resuscitating the quaint interior of the Hotel de Bourgogne Theatre was original, and the balcony scene, even in outline, enchanting. After the reading Rostand dashed off as he had come, and for many weeks I saw no more of him.

"La Princesse Lointaine was, in the meantime, produced by Sarah, first in London and then in Paris. In the English capital it was a failure; with us it gained a succes d'estime, the fantastic grace and lightness of the piece saving it from absolute shipwreck in the eyes of the literary public.

"Between ourselves," continued Coquelin, pushing aside his plate, a twinkle in his small eyes, "is the reason of this lack of success very difficult to discover? The Princess in the piece is supposed to be a fairy enchantress in her sixteenth year. The play turns on her youth and innocence. Now, honestly, is Sarah, even on the stage, any one's ideal of youth and innocence?" This was asked so naively that I burst into a laugh, in which my host joined me. Unfortunately, this grandmamma, like Ellen Terry, cannot be made to understand that there are roles she should leave alone, that with all the illusions the stage lends she can no longer play girlish parts with success.

"The failure of his play produced the most disastrous effect on Rostand, who had given up a year of his life to its composition and was profoundly chagrined by its fall. He sank into a mild melancholy, refusing for more than eighteen months to put pen to paper. On the rare occasions when we met I urged him to pull himself together and rise above disappointment. Little by little, his friends were able to awaken his dormant interest and get him to work again on Cyrano. As he slowly regained confidence and began taking pleasure once more in his work, the boyish author took to dropping in on me at impossible morning hours to read some scene hot from his ardent brain. When seated by my bedside, he declaimed his lines until, lit at his flame, I would jump out of bed, and wrapping my dressing-gown hastily around me, seize the manuscript out of his hands, and, before I knew it, find my self addressing imaginary audiences, poker in hand, in lieu of a sword, with any hat that came to handdoing duty for the plumed headgear of our hero. Little by little, line upon line, the masterpiece grew under his hands. My career as an actor has thrown me in with many forms of literary industry and dogged application, but the power of sustained effort and untiring, unflagging zeal possessed by that fragile youth surpassed anything I had seen.

"As the work began taking form, Rostand hired a place in the country, so that no visitors or invitations might tempt him away from his daily toil. Rich, young, handsome, married to a woman all Paris was admiring, with every door, social or Bohemian, wide open before his birth and talent, he voluntarily shut himself up for over a year in a dismal suburb, allowing no amusement to disturb his incessant toil. Mme. Rostand has since told me that at one time she seriously feared for his reason if not for his life, as he averaged ten hours a day steady work, and when the spell was on him would pass night after night at his study table, rewriting, cutting, modelling his play, never contented, always striving after a more expressive adjective, a more harmonious or original rhyme, casting aside a month's finished work without a second thought when he judged that another form expressed his idea more perfectly.

"That no success is cheaply bought I have long known; my profession above all others is calculated to teach one that truth.

"If Rostand's play is the best this century has produced, and our greatest critics are unanimous in pronouncing it equal, if not superior, to Victor Hugo's masterpieces, the young author has not stolen his laurels, but gained them leaf by leaf during endless midnight hours of brain-wringing effort - a price that few in a generation would be willing to give or capable of giving for fame. The labor had been in proportion to the success; it always is! I doubt if there is one word in his 'duel' ballad that has not been changed again and again for a more fitting expression, as one might assort the shades of a mosaic until a harmonious whole is produced. I have there in my desk whole scenes that he discarded because they were not essential to the action of the piece. They will probably never be printed, yet are as brilliant and cost their author as much labor as any that the public applauded to-night.

"As our rehearsals proceeded I saw another side of Rostand's character; the energy and endurance hidden in his almost effeminate frame astonished us all. He almost lived at the theatre, drilling each actor, designing each costume, ordering the setting of each scene. There was not a dress that he did not copy from some old print, or a passade that he did not indicate to the humblest member of the troop. The marvellous diction that I had noticed during the reading at Sarah's served him now and gave the key to the entire performance. I have never seen him peevish or discouraged, but always courteous and cheerful through all those weary weeks of repetition, when even the most enthusiastic feel their courage oozing away under the awful grind of afternoon and evening rehearsal, the latter beginning at midnight after the regular performance was over.

"The news was somehow spread among the theatre-loving public that something out if the ordinary was in preparation. The papers took up the tale and repeated it until the whole capital was keyed up to concert pitch. The opening night was eagerly awaited by the critics, the literary and the artistic worlds. When the curtain rose on the first act there was the emotion of a great event floating in the air." Here Coquelin's face assumed an intense expression I had rarely seen there before. He was back on the stage, living over again the glorious hours of that night's triumph. His breath was coming quick and his eyes aglow with the memory of that evening. "Never, never have I lived through such an evening. Victor Hugo's greatest triumph, the first night of Hernani, was the only theatrical event that can compare to it. It, however, was injured by the enmity of a clique who persistently hissed the new play. There is but one phrase to express the enthusiasm at our first performance - une salle en delire gives some idea of what took place. As the curtain fell on each succeeding act the entire audience would rise to its feet, shouting and cheering for ten minutes at a time. The coulisse and the dressing-rooms were packed by the critics and the author's friends, beside themselves with delight. I was trembling so I could hardly get from one costume into another, and had to refuse my door to every one. Amid all this confusion Rostand alone remained cool and seemed unconscious of his victory. He continued quietly giving last recommendations to the figurants, overseeing the setting of the scenes, and thanking the actors as they came off the stage, with the same self-possessed urbanity he had shown during the rehearsals. Finally, when the play was over, and we had time to turn and look for him, our author had disappeared, having quietly driven off with his wife to their house in the country, from which he never moved for a week."

It struck two o'clock as Coquelin ended. The sleepless city had at last gone to rest. At our feet, as we stood by the open window, the great square around the Arc de Triomphe lay silent and empty, its vast arch rising dimly against the night sky.

As I turned to go, Coquelin took my hand and remarked, smiling: "Now you have heard the story of a genius, an actor, and a masterpiece."

CHAPTER 4

MACHINE-MADE MEN

Among the commonplace white and yellow envelopes that compose the bulk of one's correspondence, appear from time to time dainty epistles on tinted paper, adorned with crests or monograms. "Ha! ha!" I think when one of these appears, "here is something worth opening!" For between ourselves, reader mine, old bachelors love to receive notes from women. It's so flattering to be remembered by the dear creatures, and recalls the time when life was beginning, and poulets in feminine writing suggested such delightful possibilities.

Only this morning an envelope of delicate Nile green caused me a distinct thrill of anticipation. To judge by appearances it could contain nothing less attractive than a declaration, so, tearing it hurriedly open, I read: "Messrs. Sparks & Splithers take pleasure in calling attention to their patent suspenders and newest designs in reversible paper collars!"

Now, if that's not enough to put any man in a bad humor for twenty-four hours, I should like to know what is? Moreover, I have "patents" in horror, experience having long ago revealed the fact that a patent is pretty sure to be only a new way of doing fast and cheaply something that formerly was accomplished slowly and well.

Few people stop to think how quickly this land of ours is degenerating into a paradise of the cheap and nasty, but allow themselves to be heated and cooled and whirled about the streets to the detriment of their nerves and digestions, under the impression that they are enjoying the benefits of modern progress.

So complex has life become in these later days that the very beds we lie on and the meals we eat are controlled by patents. Every garment and piece of furniture now pays a "royalty" to some inventor, from the hats on our heads to the carpets under foot, which latter are not only manufactured, but cleaned and shaken by machinery, and (be it remarked en passant) lose their nap prematurely in the process. To satisfy our national love of the new, an endless and nameless variety of trifles appears each season, so-called labor and time-saving combinations, that enjoy a brief hour of vogue, only to make way for a newer series of inventions.

As long as our geniuses confined themselves to making life one long and breathless scramble, it was bad enough, but a line should have been drawn where meddling with the sanctity of the toilet began. This, alas! was not done. Nothing has remained sacred to the inventor. In consequence, the average up-to-date American is a walking collection of Yankee notions, an ingenious illusion, made up of patents, requiring as nice adjustment to put together and undo as a thirteenth-century warrior, and carrying hardly less metal about his person than a Crusader of old.

There are a number of haberdashery shops on

Broadway that have caused me to waste many precious minutes gazing into their windows and wondering what the strange instruments of steel and elastic could be, that were exhibited alongside of the socks and ties. The uses of these would, in all probability, have remained wrapped in mystery but for the experience of one fateful morning (after a night in a sleeping-car), when countless hidden things were made clear, as I sat, an awestruck witness to my fellow-passengers' - toilets? - No! Getting their machinery into running order for the day, would be a more correct expression.

Originally, "tags" were the backbone of the toilet, different garments being held together by their aid. Later, buttons and attendant button-holes were evolved, now replaced by the devices used in composing the machine-made man. As far as I could see (I have overcome a natural delicacy in making my discoveries public, because it seems unfair to keep all this information to myself), nothing so archaic as a button-hole is employed at the present time by our patent-ridden compatriots. The shirt, for instance, which was formerly such a simple-minded and straightforward garment, knowing no guile, has become, in the hands of the inventors, a mere pretence, a frail scaffold, on which an elaborate superstructure of shams is erected.

The varieties of this garment that one sees in the shop windows, exposing virgin bosoms to the day, are not what they seem! Those very bosoms are fakes, and cannot open, being instead pierced by eyelets, into which bogus studs are fixed by machinery. The owner is obliged to enter into those deceptive garments surreptitiously from the rear, by stratagem, as it were. Why all this trouble, one asks, for no apparent reason, except that old-fashioned shirts opened in front, and no Yankee will wear a non-patented garment - if he can help it?

There was not a single accessory to the toilet in that car which behaved in a normal way. Buttons mostly backed into place, tail-end foremost (like horses getting between shafts), where some hidden mechanism screwed or clinched them to their moorings.

Collars and cuffs (integral parts of the primitive garment) are now a labyrinth, in which all but the initiated must lose themselves, being double-decked, detachable, reversible, and made of every known substance except linen. The cuff most in favor can be worn four different ways, and is attached to the shirt by a steel instrument three inches long, with a nipper at each end. The amount of white visible below the coat-sleeve is regulated by another contrivance, mostly of elastic, worn further up the arm, around the biceps. Modern collars are retained in position by a system of screws and levers. Socks are attached no longer with the old-fashioned garter, but by aid of a little harness similar to that worn by pug-dogs.

One traveller, after lacing his shoes, adjusted a contrivance resembling a black beetle on the knot to prevent its untying. He also wore "hygienic suspenders," a discovery of great importance (over three thousand patents have been taken out for this one necessity of the toilet!). This brace performs several tasks at the same time, such as holding unmentionable garments in place, keeping the wearer erect, and providing a night-key guard. It is also said to cure liver and kidney disease by means of an arrangement of pulleys which throw the strain according to the wearer's position - I omit the rest of its qualities!

The watches of my companions, I noticed with astonishment, all wore India-rubber ruffs around their necks. Here curiosity getting the better of discretion, I asked what purpose that invention served. It was graciously explained to me how such ruffs prevented theft. They were so made that it was impossible to draw your watch out of a pocket unless you knew the trick, which struck me as a mitigated blessing. In fact, the idea kept occurring that life might become terribly uncomfortable under these complex conditions for absent-minded people.

Pencils, I find, are no longer put into pockets or slipped behind the ear. Every commercial "gent" wears a patent on his chest, where his pen and pencil nestle in a coil of wire. Eyeglasses are not allowed to dangle aimlessly about, as of old, but retire with a snap into an oval box, after the fashion of roller shades. Scarf-pins have guards screwed on from behind, and under-garments - but here modesty stops my pen.

Seeing that I was interested in their make-up, several travelling agents on the train got out their boxes and showed me the latest artifices that could be attached to the person. One gentleman produced a collection of rings made to go on the finger with a spring, like bracelets, an arrangement, he explained, that was particularly convenient for people afflicted with enlarged joints!

Another tempted me with what he called a "literary shirt front," - it was in fact a paper pad, from which for cleanliness a leaf could be peeled each morning; the "wrong" side of the sheet thus removed contained a calendar, much useful information, and the chapters of a "continued" story, which ended when the "dickey" was used up.

A third traveller was "pushing" a collar-button that plied as many trades as Figaro, combining the functions of cravat-holder, stud, and scarf-pin. Not being successful in selling me one of these, he brought forward something "without which," he assured me, "no gentleman's wardrobe was complete"! It proved to be an insidious arrangement of gilt wire, which he adjusted on his poor, overworked collar-button, and then tied his cravat through and around it. "No tie thus made," he said, "would ever slip or get crooked." He had been so civil that it was embarrassing not to buy something of him; I invested twenty-five cents in the cravat-holder, as it seemed the least complicated of the patents on exhibition; not, however, having graduated in a school of mechanics I have never been able to make it work. It takes an hour to tie a cravat with its aid, and as long to get it untied. Most of the men in that car, I found, got around the difficulty by wearing ready-made ties which fastened behind with a clasp.

It has been suggested that the reason our compatriots have such a strained and anxious look is because they are all trying to remember the numbers of their streets and houses, the floor their office is on, and the combination of their safes. I am inclined to think that the hunted look we wear comes from an awful fear of forgetting the secrets of our patents and being unable to undo ourselves in an emergency!

Think for a moment of the horror of coming home tired and sleepy after a convivial evening, and finding that some of your hidden machinery had gone wrong;

that by a sudden movement you had disturbed the nice balance of some lever which in revenge refused to release its prey! The inventors of one well-known cuff-holder claim that it had a "bull-dog grip." Think of sitting dressed all night in the embrace of that mechanical canine until the inventor could be called in to set you free!

I never doubted that bravery was the leading characteristic of the American temperament; since that glimpse into the secret composition of my compatriots, admiration has been vastly increased. The foolhardy daring it must require - dressed as those men were - to go out in a thunder-storm makes one shudder: it certainly could not be found in any other race. The danger of cross-country hunting or bull-fighting is as nothing compared to the risk a modern American takes when he sits in a trolley-car, where the chances of his machinery forming a fatal "short circuit" must be immense. The utter impossibility in which he finds himself of making a toilet quickly on account of so many time-saving accessories must increase his chances of getting "left" in an accident about fifty per cent. Who but one of our people could contemplate with equanimity the thought of attempting the adjustment of such delicate and difficult combinations while a steamer was sinking and the life-boats being manned?

Our grandfathers contributed the wooden nutmeg to civilization, and endowed a grateful universe with other money-saving devices. To-day the inventor takes the American baby from his cradle and does not release him even at the grave. What a treat one of the machine-made men of to-day will be to the archeologists of the year 3000, when they chance upon a well-preserved specimen, with all his patents thick upon I him! With a prophetic eye one can almost see the kindly old gentleman of that day studying the paraphernalia found in the tomb and attempting to account for the different pieces. Ink will flow and discussions rage between the camp maintaining that cuff-holders were tutelar deities buried with the dead by pious relatives and the croup asserting that the little pieces of steel were a form of pocket money in the year 1900. Both will probably misquote Tennyson and Kipling in support of their theories.

The question has often been raised, What side of our nineteenth-century civilization will be most admired by future generations? In view of the above facts there can remain little doubt that when the secrets of the paper collar and the trouser-stretcher have become lost arts, it will be those benefits that remote ages will envy us, and rare specimens of "ventilated shoes" and "reversible tissue-paper undergarments" will form the choicest treasures of the collector.

CHAPTER 5

PARNASSUS

Many years ago, a gentleman with whom I was driving in a distant quarter of Paris took me to a house on the rue Montparnasse, where we remained an hour or more, he chatting with its owner, and I listening to their conversation, and wondering at the confusion of books in the big room. As we drove away, my companion turned to me and said, "Don't forget this afternoon. You have seen one of the greatest writers our century has produced, although the world does not yet realize it. You will learn to love his works when you are older, and it will be a satisfaction to remember that you saw and spoke with him in the flesh! "

When I returned later to Paris the little house had changed hands, and a marble tablet stating that Sainte-Beuve had lived and died there adorned its facade. My student footsteps took me many times through that quiet street, but never without a vision of the poet-critic flashing back, as I glanced up at the window where he had stood and talked with us; as my friend predicted, Sainte-Beuve's writings had become a precious part of my small library, the memory of his genial face adding a vivid interest to their perusal.

I made a little Pilgrimage recently to the quiet old

garden where, after many years' delay, a bust of this writer has been unveiled, with the same companion, now very old, who thirty years ago presented me to the original.

There is, perhaps, in all Paris no more exquisite corner than the Garden of the Luxembourg. At every season it is beautiful. The winter sunlight seems to linger on its stately Italian terraces after it has ceased to shine elsewhere. The first lilacs bloom here in the spring, and when midsummer has turned all the rest of Paris into a blazing, white wilderness, these gardens remain cool and tranquil in the heart of turbulent "Bohemia," a bit of fragrant nature filled with the song of birds and the voices of children. Surely it was a gracious inspiration that selected this shady park as the "Poets' Corner" of great, new Paris. Henri Murger, Leconte de Lisle, Theodore de Banville, Paul Verlaine, are here, and now Sainte-Beuve has come back to his favorite haunt. Like Francois Coppee and Victor Hugo, he loved these historic allees, and knew the stone in them as he knew the "Latin Quater," for his life was passed between the bookstalls of the quays and the outlying street where he lived.

As we sat resting in the shade, my companion, who had been one of Sainte-Beuve's pupils, fell to talking of his master, his memory refreshed by the familiar surroundings. "Can anything be sadder," he said, "than finding a face one has loved turned into stone, or names that were the watchwords of one's youth serving as signs at street corners - la rue Flaubert or Theodore de Banville? How far away they make the past seem! Poor Sainte-Beuve, that bust yonder is but a poor reward for a life of toil, a modest tribute to his encyclopaedic brain! His works, however, are his best monument; he would be the last to repine or cavil.

"The literary world of my day had two poles, between which it vibrated. The little house in the rue Montparnasse was one, the rock of Guernsey the other. We spoke with awe of 'Father Hugo' and mentioned 'Uncle Beuve' with tenderness. The Goncourt brothers accepted Sainte-Beuve's judgment on their work as the verdict of a 'Supreme Court.' Not a poet or author of that day but climbed with a beating heart the narrow staircase that led to the great writer's library. Paul Verlaine regarded as his literary diploma a letter from this 'Balzac de la critique.' "

"At the entrance of the quaint Passage du Commerce, under the arch that leads into the rue Saint-Andre-des-Arts, stands a hotel, where for years Sainte-Beuve came daily to work (away from the importunate who besieged his dwelling) in a room hired under the assumed name of Delorme. It was there that we sent him a basket of fruit one morning addressed to Mr. Delorme, ne Sainte-Beuve. It was there that most of his enormous labor was accomplished.

"A curious corner of old Paris that Cour du Commerce! Just opposite his window was the apartment where Danton lived. If one chose to seek for them it would not be hard to discover on the pavement of this same passage the marks made by a young doctor in decapitating sheep with his newly invented machine. The doctor's name was Guillotin.

"The great critic loved these old quarters filled with history. He was fond of explaining that Montparnasse had been a hill where the students of the seventeenth and eighteenth centuries came to amuse themselves. In

1761 the slope was levelled and the boulevard laid out, but the name was predestined, he would declare, for the habitation of the 'Parnassiens.'

"His enemies pretended that you had but to mention Michelet, Balzac, and Victor Hugo to see Sainte-Beuve in three degrees of rage. He had, it is true, distinct expressions on hearing those authors discussed. The phrase then much used in speaking of an original personality, 'He is like a character out of Balzac,' always threw my master into a temper. I cannot remember, however, having seen him in one of those famous rages which made Barbey d'Aurevilly say that 'Sainte-Beuve was a clever man with the temper of a turkey!' The former was much nearer the truth when he called the author of Les Lundis a French Wordsworth, or compared him to a lay benedictin. He had a way of reading a newly acquired volume as he walked through the streets that was typical of his life. My master was always studying and always advancing.

"He never entirely recovered from his mortification at being hissed by the students on the occasion of his first lecture at the College de France. Returning home he loaded two pistols, one for the first student who should again insult him, and the other to blow out his own brains. It was no idle threat. The man Guizot had nicknamed 'Werther' was capable of executing his plan, for this causeless unpopularity was anguish to him. After his death, I found those two pistols loaded in his bedroom, but justice had been done another way. All opposition had vanished. Every student in the 'Quarter' followed the modest funeral of their Senator, who had become the champion of literary liberty in an epoch when poetry was held in chains.

"The Empire which made him Senator gained, however, but an indocile recruit. On his one visit to Compiegne in 1863, the Emperor, wishing to be particularly gracious, said to him, 'I always read the Moniteur on Monday, when your article appears.' Unfortunately for this compliment, it was the Constitutionnel that had been publishing the Nouveaux Lundis for more than four years. In spite of the united efforts of his friends, Sainte-Beuve could not be brought to the point of complimenting Napoleon III. on his Life of Caesar.

The author of Les Consolations remained through life the proudest and most independent of men, a bourgeois, enemy of all tyranny, asking protection of no one. And what a worker! Reading, sifting, studying, analyzing his subject before composing one of his famous Lundis, a literary portrait which he aimed at making complete and final. One of these articles cost him as much labor as other authors give to the composition of a volume.

"By way of amusement on Sunday evenings, when work was temporarily laid aside, he loved the theatre, delighting in every kind of play, from the broad farces of the Palais Royal to the tragedies of Racine, and entertaining comedians in order, as he said, 'to keep young'! One evening Theophile Gautier brought a pretty actress to dinner. Sainte-Beuve, who was past-master in the difficult art of conversation, and on whom a fair woman acted as an inspiration, surpassed himself on this occasion, surprising even the Goncourts with his knowledge of the Eighteenth century and the women of that time, Mme. de Boufflers, Mlle. de Lespinasse, la Marechale de Luxembourg. The hours flew by unheeded by all of his guests but one. The debutante was overheard confiding, later in the evening, to a friend at the Gymnase, where she performed in the last act, 'Ouf! I'm glad to get here. I've been dining with a stupid old Senator. They told me he would be amusing, but I've been bored to death.' Which reminded me of my one visit to England, when I heard a young nobleman declare that he had been to 'such a dull dinner to meet a duffer called "Renan!" '

"Sainte-Beuve's Larmes de Racine was given at the Theatre Francais during its author's last illness. His disappointment at not seeing the performance was so keen that M. Thierry, then administrateur of La Comedie, took Mlle. Favart to the rue Montparnasse, that she might recite his verses to the dying writer. When the actress, then in the zenith of her fame and beauty, came to the lines -

> *Jean Racine, le grand poete,*
> *Le poete aimant et pieux,*
> *Apres que sa lyre muette*
> *Se fut voilee a tous les yeux,*
> *Renoncant a la gloire humaine,*
> *S'il sentait en son ame pleine*
> *Le flot contenu murmurer,*
> *Ne savait que fondre en priere,*
> *Pencher l'urne dans la poussiere*
> *Aux pieds du Seigneur, et pleurer!*

the tears of Sainte-Beuve accompanied those of Racine!"

There were tears also in the eyes my companion turned toward me as he concluded. The sun had set while he had been speaking. The marble of the statues gleamed white against the shadows of the sombre old garden. The guardians were closing the gates and warning the lingering visitors as we strolled toward the entrance.

It seemed as if we had been for an hour in the presence of the portly critic; and the circle of brilliant men and witty women who surrounded him - Flaubert, Tourgueneff, Theophile Gautier, Renan, George Sand - were realities at that moment, not abstractions with great names. It was like returning from another age, to step out again into the glare and bustle of the Boulevard St. Michel.

CHAPTER 6

MODERN ARCHITECTURE

If a foreign tourist, ignorant of his whereabouts, were to sail about sunset up our spacious bay and view for the first time the eccentric sky-line of lower New York, he would rub his eyes and wonder if they were not playing him a trick, for distance and twilight lend the chaotic masses around the Battery a certain wild grace suggestive of Titan strongholds or prehistoric abodes of Wotan, rather than the business part of a practical modern city.

"But," as John Drew used to say in The Masked Ball, "what a difference in the morning!" when a visit to his banker takes the new arrival down to Wall Street, and our uncompromising American daylight dispels his illusions.

Years ago SPIRITUAL Arthur Gilman mourned over the decay of architecture in New York and pointed out that Stewart's shop, at Tenth Street, bore about the same relation to Ictinus' noble art as an iron cooking stove! It is well death removed the Boston critic before our city entered into its present Brobdingnagian phase. If he considered that Stewart's and the Fifth Avenue Hotel failed in artistic beauty, what would have been his opinion of the graceless piles that crowd our island to-day, beside which those older buildings seem almost classical in their simplicity?

One hardly dares to think what impression a student familiar with the symmetry of Old World structures must receive on arriving for the first time, let us say, at the Bowling Green, for the truth would then dawn upon him that what appeared from a distance to be the ground level of the island was in reality the roof line of average four-story buildings, from among which the keeps and campaniles that had so pleased him (when viewed from the Narrows) rise like gigantic weeds gone to seed in a field of grass.

It is the heterogeneous character of the buildings down town that renders our streets so hideous. Far from seeking harmony, builders seem to be trying to "go" each other "one story better"; if they can belittle a neighbor in the process it is clear gain, and so much advertisement. Certain blocks on lower Broadway are gems in this way! Any one who has glanced at an auctioneer's shelves when a "job lot" of books is being sold, will doubtless have noticed their resemblance to the sidewalks of our down town streets. Dainty little duodecimo buildings are squeezed in between towering in-folios, and richly bound and tooled octavos chum with cheap editions. Our careless City Fathers have not even given themselves the trouble of pushing their stone and brick volumes into the same line, but allow them to straggle along the shelf - I beg pardon, the sidewalk - according to their own sweet will.

The resemblance of most new business buildings to flashy books increases the more one studies them; they have the proportions of school atlases, and, like them, are adorned only on their backs (read fronts). The modern builder, like the frugal binder, leaves the sides of his creations unadorned, and expends his ingenuity in decorating the narrow strip which he naively imagines will be the only part seen, calmly ignoring the fact that on glancing up or down a street the sides of houses are what we see first. It is almost impossible to get mathematically opposite a building, yet that is the only point from which these new constructions are not grotesque.

It seems as though the rudiments of common sense would suggest that under existing circumstances the less decoration put on a facade the greater would be the harmony of the whole. But trifles like harmony and fitness are splendidly ignored by the architects of to-day, who, be it remarked in passing, have slipped into another curious habit for which I should greatly like to see an explanation offered. As long as the ground floors and the tops of their creations are elaborate, the designer evidently thinks the intervening twelve or fifteen stories can shift for themselves. One clumsy mass on the Bowling Green is an excellent example of this weakness. Its ground floor is a playful reproduction of the tombs of Egypt. About the second story the architect must have become discouraged - or perhaps the owner's funds gave out - for the next dozen floors are treated in the severest "tenement house" manner; then, as his building terminates well up in the sky, a top floor or two are, for no apparent reason, elaborately adorned. Indeed, this desire for a brilliant finish pervades the neighborhood. The Johnson Building on Broad Street (to choose one out of the many) is sober and discreet in design for a dozen stories, but bursts at its top into a Byzantine colonnade. Why? one asks in wonder.

Eliot Gregory

Another new-comer, corner of Wall and Nassau Streets, is a commonplace structure, with a fairly good cornice, on top of which - an afterthought, probably - a miniature State Capitol has been added, with dome and colonnade complete. The result recalls dear, absent-minded Miss Matty (in Mrs. Gaskell's charming story), when she put her best cap on top of an old one and sat smiling at her visitors from under the double headdress!

Nowhere in the world - not even in Moscow, that city of domes - can one see such a collection of pagodas, cupolas, kiosks, and turrets as grace the roofs of our office buildings! Architects evidently look upon such adornments as compensations! The more hideous the structure, the finer its dome! Having perpetrated a blot upon the city that cries to heaven in its enormity, the repentant owner adds a pagoda or two, much in the same spirit, doubtless, as prompts an Italian peasant to hang a votive heart on some friendly shrine when a crime lies heavy on his conscience.

What would be thought of a book-collector who took to standing inkstands or pepperboxes on the tops of his tallest volumes by way of adornment? Yet domes on business buildings are every bit as appropriate. A choice collection of those monstrosities graces Park Row, one much-gilded offender varying the monotony by looking like a yellow stopper in a high-shouldered bottle! How modern architects with the exquisite City Hall before them could have wandered so far afield in their search for the original must always remain a mystery.

When a tall, thin building happens to stand on a corner, the likeness to an atlas is replaced by a grotesque resemblance to a waffle iron, of which one structure just finished on Rector Street skilfully reproduces' the lines. The rows of little windows were evidently arranged to imitate the indentations on that humble utensil, and the elevated road at the back seems in this case to do duty as the handle. Mrs. Van Rensselaer tells us in her delightful Goede Vrouw of Mana-ha-ta that waffle irons used to be a favorite wedding present among the Dutch settlers of this island, and were adorned with monograms and other devices, so perhaps it is atavism that makes us so fond of this form in building! As, however, no careful Hausfrau would have stood her iron on its edge, architects should hesitate before placing their buildings in that position, as the impression of instability is the same in each case.

After leaving the vicinity of the City Hall, the tall slabs that like magnified milestones mark the progress of Architecture up Broadway become a shade less objectionable, although one meets some strange freaks in so-called decoration by the way. Why, for instance, were those Titan columns grouped around the entrance to the American Surety Company's building? They do not support anything (the "business" of columns in architecture) except some rather feeble statuary, and do seriously block the entrance. Were they added with the idea of fitness? That can hardly be, for a portico is as inappropriate to such a building as it would be to a parlor car, and almost as inconvenient.

Farther up town our attention is arrested by another misplaced adornment. What purpose can that tomb with a railing round it serve on top of the New York Life Insurance building? It looks like a monument in Greenwood, surmounted by a rat-trap, but no one is interred there, and vermin can hardly be troublesome at that altitude.

How did this craze for decoration originate? The inhabitants of Florence and Athens did not consider it necessary. There must, I feel sure, be a reason for its use in this city; American land-lords rarely spend money without a purpose; perhaps they find that rococo detail draws business and inspires confidence!

I should like to ask the architects of New York one question: Have they not been taught that in their art, as in every other, pretences are vulgar, that things should be what they seem? Then why do they continue to hide steel and fire-brick cages under a veneer of granite six inches thick, causing them to pose as solid stone buildings? If there is a demand for tall, light structures, why not build them simply (as bridges are constructed), and not add a poultice of bogus columns and zinc cornices that serve no purpose and deceive no one?

Union Square possesses blocks out of which the Jackson and Decker buildings spring with a noble disregard of all rules and a delicious incongruity that reminds one of Falstaff's corps of ill-drilled soldiers. Madison Square, however, is facile princeps, with its annex to the Hoffman House, a building which would make the fortune of any dime museum that could fence it in and show it for a fee! Long contemplation of this structure from my study window has printed every comic detail on my brain. It starts off at the ground level to be an imitation of the Doge's Palace (a neat and appropriate idea in itself for a Broadway shop). At the second story, following the usual New York method, it reverts to a design suggestive of a county jail (the Palace and the Prison), with here and there a balcony hung out, emblematical, doubtless, of the inmates' wash and bedding. At the ninth floor the repentant architect adds two more stories in memory of the Doge's residence. Have you ever seen an accordion (concertina, I believe, is the correct name) hanging in a shop window? The Twenty-fifth Street Doge's Palace reminds me of that humble instrument. The wooden part, where the keys and round holes are, stands on the sidewalk. Then come an indefinite number of pleats, and finally the other wooden end well up among the clouds. So striking is this resemblance that at times one expects to hear the long-drawn moans peculiar to the concertina issuing from those portals. Alas! even the most original designs have their drawbacks! After the proprietor of the Venetian accordion had got his instrument well drawn out and balanced on its end, he perceived that it dwarfed the adjacent buildings, so cast about in his mind for a scheme to add height and dignity to the rest of the block. One day the astonished neighborhood saw what appeared to be a "roomy suburban villa" of iron rising on the roof of the old Hoffman House. The results suggests a small man who, being obliged to walk with a giant, had put on a hat several times too large in order to equalize their heights!

How astonished Pericles and his circle of architects and sculptors would be could they stand on the corner of Broadway and Twenty-eighth Street and see the miniature Parthenon that graces the roof of a pile innocent of other Greek ornament? They would also recognize their old friends, the ladies of the Erechtheum, doing duty on the Reveillon Building across the way, pretending to hold up a cornice, which, being in proportion to the building, is several hundred times too big for them to carry. They can't be seen from the sidewalk, - the street is too narrow for that, - but such trifles don't deter builders from decorating when the fit is on them. Perhaps this one got his caryatides at a bargain, and had to work them in somewhere; so it is not fair to be hard on him.

If ever we take to ballooning, all these elaborate tops may add materially to our pleasure. At the present moment the birds, and angels, it is to be hoped, appreciate the effort. I, perhaps, of all the inhabitants of the city, have seen those ladies face to face, when I have gone on a semi-monthly visit to my roof to look for leaks!

"It's all very well to carp and cavil," many readers will say, "but 'Idler' forgets that our modern architects have had to contend with difficulties that the designers of other ages never faced, demands for space and light forcing the nineteenth-century builders to produce structures which they know are neither graceful nor in proportion!"

If my readers will give themselves the trouble to glance at several office buildings in the city, they will realize that the problem is not without a solution. In almost every case where the architect has refrained from useless decoration and stuck to simple lines, the result, if not beautiful, has at least been inoffensive. It is where inappropriate elaboration is added that taste is offended. Such structures as the Singer building, corner of Liberty Street and Broadway, and the home of Life, in Thirty-first Street, prove that beauty and grace of facade can be adapted to modern business wants.

Feeling as many New Yorkers do about this defacing of what might have been the most beautiful of modern cities, it is galling to be called upon to admire where it is already an effort to tolerate.

A sprightly gentleman, writing recently in a scientific weekly, goes into ecstasies of admiration over the advantages and beauty of a steel mastodon on Park Row, a building that has the proportions of a carpenter's plane stood on end, decorated here and there with balconies and a colonnade perched on brackets up toward its fifteenth story. He complacently gives us its weight and height as compared with the pyramids, and numerous other details as to floor space and ventilation, and hints in conclusion that only old fogies and dullards, unable to keep pace with the times, fail to appreciate the charm of such structures in a city. One of the "points" this writer makes is the quality of air enjoyed by tenants, amusingly oblivious of the fact that at least three facades of each tall building will see the day only so long as the proprietors of adjacent land are too poor or too busy to construct similar colossi!

When all the buildings in a block are the same height, seven eighths of the rooms in each will be without light or ventilation. It's rather poor taste to brag of advantages that are enjoyed only through the generosity of one's neighbors.

Business demands may force us to bow before the necessity of these horrors, but it certainly is "rubbing it in" to ask our applause. When the Eiffel Tower was in course of construction, the artists and literary lights of Paris raised a tempest of protest. One wonders why so little of the kind has been done here. It is perhaps rather late in the day to suggest reform, yet if more

New Yorkers would interest themselves in the work, much might still be done to modify and improve our metropolis.

One hears with satisfaction that a group of architects have lately met and discussed plans for the embellishment of our neglected city. There is a certain poetical justice in the proposition coming from those who have worked so much of the harm. Remorse has before now been known to produce good results. The United States treasury yearly receives large sums of "conscience money."

CHAPTER 7

WORLDLY COLOR-BLINDNESS

Myriads of people have no ear for music and derive but little pleasure from sweet sounds. Strange as it may appear, many gifted and sensitive mortals have been unable to distinguish one note from another, Apollo's harmonious art remaining for them, as for the elder Dumas, only an "expensive noise."

Another large class find it impossible to discriminate between colors. Men afflicted in this way have even become painters of reputation. I knew one of the latter, who, when a friend complimented him on having caught the exact shade of a pink toilet in one of his portraits, answered, "Does that dress look pink to you? I thought it was green!" and yet he had copied what he saw correctly.

Both these classes are to be pitied, but are not the cause of much suffering to others. It is annoying, I grant you, to be torn asunder in a collision, because red and green lights on the switches combined into a pleasing harmony before the brakeman's eyes. The tone-deaf gentleman who insists on whistling a popular melody is almost as trying as the lady suffering from the same weakness, who shouts, "Ninon, Ninon, que fais-tu de la vie!" until you feel impelled to cry, "Que faites-vous, madame, with the key?"

Examinations now keep daltonic gentlemen out of locomotives, and ladies who have lost their "keys" are apt to find their friends' pianos closed. What we cannot guard against is a variety of the genus homo which suffers from "social color-blindness." These well-meaning mortals form one of the hardest trials that society is heir to; for the disease is incurable, and as it is almost impossible to escape from them, they continue to spread dismay and confusion along their path to the bitter end.

This malady, which, as far as I know, has not been diagnosed, invades all circles, and is, curiously enough, rampant among well-born and apparently well-bred people.

Why is it that the entertainments at certain houses are always dull failures, while across the way one enjoys such agreeable evenings? Both hosts are gentlemen, enjoying about the same amount of "unearned increment," yet the atmosphere of their houses is radically different. This contrast cannot be traced to the dulness or brilliancy of the entertainer and his wife. Neither can it be laid at the door of inexperience, for the worst offenders are often old hands at the game.

The only explanation possible is that the owners of houses where one is bored are socially color-blind, as cheerfully unconscious of their weakness as the keyless lady and the whistling abomination.

Since increasing wealth has made entertaining general and lavish, this malady has become more and more apparent, until one is tempted to parody Mme.

Roland's dying exclamation and cry, "Hospitality! hospitility! what crimes are committed in thy name!"

Entertaining is for many people but an excuse for ostentation. For others it is a means to an end; while a third variety apparently keep a debit and credit account with their acquaintances - in books of double entry, so that no errors may occur - and issue invitations like receipts, only in return for value received.

We can rarely tell what is passing in the minds of people about us. Some of those mentioned above may feel a vague pleasure when their rooms are filled with a chattering crowd of more or less well-assorted guests; if that is denied them, can find consolation for the outlay in an indefinite sensation of having performed a duty, - what duty, or to whom, they would, however, find it difficult to define.

Let the novice flee from the allurements of such a host. Old hands know him and have got him on their list, escaping when escape is possible; for he will mate the green youth with the red frump, or like a premature millennium force the lion and the lamb to lie down together, and imagine he has given unmixed pleasure to both.

One would expect that great worldly lights might learn by experience how fatal bungled entertainments can be, but such is not the case. Many well-intentioned people continue sacrificing their friends on the altar of hospitality year after year with never a qualm of conscience or a sensation of pity for their victims. One practical lady of my acquaintance asks her guests alphabetically, commencing the season and the first leaf of her visiting list simultaneously and working steadily on through both to "finis." If you are an A, you will meet only A's at her table, with perhaps one or two B's thrown in to fill up; you may sit next to your mother-in-law for all the hostess cares. She has probably never heard that the number of guests at table should not exceed that of the muses; or if by any chance she has heard it, does not care, and considers such a rule old-fashioned and not appropriate to our improved modern methods of entertaining.

One wonders what possible satisfaction a host can derive from providing fifty people with unwholesome food and drink at a fixed date. It is a physical impossibility for him to have more than a passing word with his guests, and ten to one the unaccustomed number has upset the internal arrangements of his household, so that the dinner will, in consequence, be poor and the service defective.

A side-light on this question came to me recently when an exceedingly frank husband confided to a circle of his friends at the club the scheme his wife, who, though on pleasure bent, was of a frugal mind, had adopted to balance her social ledger.

"As we dine out constantly through the year," remarked Benedict, "some return is necessary. So we wait until the height of the winter season, when everybody is engaged two weeks in advance, then send out our invitations at rather short notice for two or three consecutive dinners. You'd be surprised," he remarked, with a beaming smile, "what a number refuse; last winter we cancelled all our obligations with two dinners, the flowers and entrees being as fresh on the second evening as the first! It's wonderful!" he remarked in conclusion, "how simple entertaining becomes when one knows how!" Which reminded me of an ingenious youth I once heard telling some friends how easy he had found it to write the book he had just published. After his departure we agreed that if he found it so easy it would not be worth our while to read his volume.

Tender-hearted people generally make bad hosts. They have a way of collecting the morally lame, halt, and blind into their drawing-rooms that gives those apartments the air of a convalescent home. The moment a couple have placed themselves beyond the social pale, these purblind hosts conceive an affection for and lavish hospitality upon them. If such a host has been fortunate enough to get together a circle of healthy people, you may feel confident that at the last moment a leper will be introduced. This class of entertainers fail to see that society cannot he run on a philanthropic basis, and so insist on turning their salons into hospitals.

It would take too long to enumerate the thousand idiosyncrasies of the color-blind; few, however, are more amusing than those of the impulsive gentlemen who invite people to their homes indiscriminately, because they happen to feel in a good humor or chance to be seated next them at another house, - invitations which the host regrets half an hour later, and would willingly recall. "I can't think why I asked the So-and-sos!" he will confide to you. "I can't abide them; they are as dull as the dropsy!" Many years ago in Paris, we used to call a certain hospitable lady's invitations "soup tickets," so little individuality did they possess.

The subtle laws of moral precedence are difficult reading for the most intelligent, and therefore remain sealed books to the afflicted mortals mentioned here. The delicate tact that, with no apparent effort, combines congenial elements into a delightful whole is lacking in their composition. The nice discrimination that presides over some households is replaced by a jovial indifference to other persons' feelings and prejudices.

The idea of placing pretty Miss Debutante next young Strongboys instead of giving her over into the clutches of old Mr. Boremore will never enter these obtuse entertainers' heads, any more than that of trying to keep poor, defenceless Mrs. Mouse out of young Tom Cat's claws.

It is useless to enumerate instances; people have suffered too severely at the hands of careless and incompetent hosts not to know pretty well what the title of this paper means. So many of us have come away from fruitless evenings, grinding our teeth, and vowing never to enter those doors again while life lasts, that the time seems ripe for a protest.

If the color-blind would only refrain from painting, and the tone-deaf not insist on inviting one to their concerts, the world would be a much more agreeable place. If people would only learn what they can and what they can't do, and leave the latter feats alone, a vast amount of unnecessary annoyance would be avoided and the tiresome old grindstone turn to a more cheerful tune.

CHAPTER 8

IDLING IN MID-OCEAN

To those fortunate mortals from whom Poseidon exacts no tribute in crossing his broad domain, a transatlantic voyage must afford each year an ever new delight. The cares and worries of existence fade away and disappear in company with the land, in the deep bosom of the ocean buried. One no longer feels like the bored mortal who has all winter turned the millstone of work and pleasure, but seems to have transmigrated into a new body, endowed with a ravenous appetite and perfectly fresh sensations.

Perhaps it is only the novelty of the surroundings; but as I lie somnolent in my chair, tucked into a corner of the white deck, watching the jade-colored water rush past below, and the sea-gulls circle gayly overhead, the summum bonum of earthly contentment seems attained. The book chosen with care remains uncut; the sense of physical and mental rest is too exquisite to be broken by any effort, even the reading of a favorite author.

Drowsy lapses into unconsciousness obscure the senses, like the transparent clouds that from time to time dim the sunlight. A distant bell in the wheel-house chimes the lazy half-hours. Groups of people come and go like figures on a lantern-slide. A curiously detached reeling makes the scene and the actors in it as unreal as a painted ship manned by a shadowy crew. The inevitable child tumbles on its face and is picked up shrieking by tender parents; energetic youths organize games of skill or discover whales on the horizon, without disturbing one's philosophic calm.

I congratulate myself on having chosen a foreign line. For a week at least no familiar name will be spoken, no accustomed face appear. The galling harness of routine is loosened; one breathes freely again conscious of the unoccupied hours in perspective.

The welcome summons to luncheon comes as a pleasant shock. Is it possible that the morning has passed? It seems to have but commenced. I rouse myself and descend to the cabin. Toward the end of the meal a rubicund Frenchman opposite makes the startling proposition that if I wish to send a message home he will undertake to have it delivered. It is not until I notice the little square of oiled paper he is holding out to me that I understand this reference to the "pigeon post" with which the Compagnie Transatlantique is experimenting. At the invitation of this new acquaintance I ascend to the upper deck and watch his birds depart.

The tiny bits of paper on which we have written (post-card fashion) message and address are rolled two or three together, and inserted into a piece of quill less than two inches long, which, however, they do not entirely fill. While a pigeon is held by one man, another pushes one of the bird's tail-feathers well through the quill, which is then fastened in its place by two minute wooden wedges. A moment later the pigeon is tossed up into the air, and we witness the working of that mysterious instinct which all our modern science leaves unexplained. After a turn or two far up in the clear sky, the bird gets its bearings and darts off on its five-hundred-mile journey across unknown seas to an unseen land - a voyage that no deviation or loitering will lengthen, and only fatigue or accident interrupt, until he alights at his cote.

Five of these willing messengers were started the first day out, and five more will leave to-morrow, poor little aerial postmen, almost predestined to destruction (in the latter case), for we shall then be so far from land that their one chance of life and home must depend on finding some friendly mast where an hour's rest may be taken before the bird starts again on his journey.

In two or three days, according to the weather, we shall begin sending French pigeons on ahead of us toward Havre. The gentleman in charge of them tells me that his wife received all the messages he sent to her during his westward trip, the birds appearing each morning at her window (where she was in the habit feeding them) with their tidings from mid-ocean. He also tells me that the French fleet in the Mediterranean recently received messages from their comrades in the Baltic on the third day by these feathered envoys.

It is hoped that in future ocean steamers will be able to keep up communication with the land at least four out of the seven days of their trips, so that, in case of delay or accident, their exact position and circumstances can be made known at headquarters. It is a pity, the originator of the scheme remarked, that sea-gulls are such hopeless vagabonds, for they can fly much greater distances than pigeons, and are not affected by dampness, which seriously cripples the present messengers.

Later in the day a compatriot, inspired doubtless by the morning's experiment, confided to me that he had hit on "a great scheme," which he intends to develop on arriving. His idea is to domesticate families of porpoises at Havre and New York, as that fish passes for having (like the pigeon) the homing instinct. Ships provided with the parent fish can free one every twenty-four hours, charged with the morning's mail. The inventor of this luminous idea has already designed the letter-boxes that are to be strapped on the fishes' backs, and decided on a neat uniform for his postmen.

It is amusing during the first days "out" to watch the people whom chance has thrown together into such close quarters. The occult power that impels a pigeon to seek its kind is feeble in comparison with the faculty that travellers develop under these circumstances for seeking out congenial spirits. Twelve hours do not pass before affinities draw together; what was apparently a homogeneous mass has by that time grouped and arranged itself into three or four distinct circles.

The "sporty" gentlemen in loud clothes have united in the bonds of friendship with the travelling agents and have chosen the smoking-room as their headquarters. No mellow sunset or serene moonlight will tempt these comrades from the subtleties of poker; the pool on the run is the event of their day.

A portly prima donna is the centre of another circle. Her wraps, her dogs, her admirers, and her brand-new husband (a handsome young Hungarian with a voice like two Bacian bulls) fill the sitting-room, where the piano gets but little rest. Neither sunshine nor soft winds can draw them to the deck. Although too ill for the regular meals, this group eat and drink during fifteen out of the twenty-four hours.

The deck, however, is not deserted; two fashionable dressmakers revel there. These sociable ladies asked the commissaire at the start "to introduce all the young unmarried men to them," as they wanted to be jolly. They have a numerous court around them, and champagne, like the conversation, flows freely. These ladies have already become expert at shuffleboard, but their "sea legs" are not so good as might be expected, and the dames require to be caught and supported by their admirers at each moment to prevent them from tripping - an immense joke, to judge by the peals of laughter that follow.

The American wife of a French ambassador sits on the captain's right. A turn of the diplomatic wheel is taking the lady to Madrid, where her position will call for supreme tact and self-restraint. One feels a thrill of national pride on looking at her high-bred young face and listening as she chats in French and Spanish, and wonders once more at the marvellous faculty our women have of adapting themselves so graciously and so naturally to difficult positions, which the women of other nations rarely fill well unless born to the purple. It is the high opinion I have of my countrywomen that has made me cavil, before now, on seeing them turned into elaborately dressed nullities by foolish and too adoring husbands.

The voyage is wearing itself away. Sunny days are succeeded by gray mornings, as exquisite in their way, when one can feel the ship fight against contending wind and wave, and shiver under the blows received in a struggle which dashes the salt spray high over the decks. There is an aroma in the air then that breathes new life into jaded nerves, and stirs the drop of old Norse blood, dormant in most American veins, into quivering ecstasy. One dreams of throwing off the trammels of civilized existence and returning to the free life of older days.

But here is Havre glittering in the distance against her background of chalk cliffs. People come on deck in strangely conventional clothes and with demure citified airs. Passengers of whose existence you were unaware suddenly make their appearance. Two friends meet near me for the first time. "Hallo, Jones!" says one of them, "are you crossing?"

"Yes," answers Jones, "are you?"

The company's tug has come alongside by this time, bringing its budget of letters and telegrams. The brief holiday is over. With a sigh one comes back to the positive and the present, and patiently resumes the harness of life.

CHAPTER 9

"CLIMBERS" IN ENGLAND

The expression "Little Englander," much used of late to designate an inhabitant of the Mother Isle in contra-distinction to other subjects of Her Majesty, expresses neatly the feeling of our insular cousins not only as regards ourselves, but also the position affected toward their colonial brothers and sisters.

Have you ever noticed that in every circle there is some individual assuming to do things better than his comrades - to know more, dress better, run faster, pronounce more correctly? Who, unless promptly suppressed, will turn the conversation into a monologue relating to his own exploits and opinions. To differ is to bring down his contempt upon your devoted head! To argue is time wasted!

Human nature is, however, so constituted that a man of this type mostly succeeds in hypnotizing his hearers into sharing his estimate of himself, and impressing upon them the conviction that he is a rare being instead of a commonplace mortal. He is not a bad sort of person at bottom, and ready to do one a friendly turn - if it does not entail too great inconvenience. In short, a good fellow, whose principal defect is the profound conviction that he was born superior to the rest of mankind.

What this individual is to his environment, Englishmen are to the world at large. It is the misfortune, not the fault, of the rest of the human race, that they are not native to his island; a fact, by the way, which outsiders are rarely allowed to lose sight of, as it entails a becoming modesty on their part.

Few idiosyncrasies get more quickly on American nerves or are further from our hearty attitude toward strangers. As we are far from looking upon wandering Englishmen with suspicion, it takes us some time to realize that Americans who cut away from their countrymen and settle far from home are regarded with distrust and reluctantly received. When a family of this kind prepares to live in their neighborhood, Britons have a formula of three questions they ask themselves concerning the new-comers: "Whom do they know? How much are they worth?" and "What amusement (or profit) are we likely to get out of them?" If the answer to all or any of the three queries is satisfactory, my lord makes the necessary advances and becomes an agreeable, if not a witty or original, companion.

Given this and a number of other peculiarities, it seems curious that a certain class of Americans should be so anxious to live in England. What is it tempts them? It cannot be the climate, for that is vile; nor the city of London, for it is one of the ugliest in existence; nor their "cuisine" - for although we are not good cooks ourselves, we know what good food is and could give Britons points. Neither can it be art, nor the opera, - one finds both better at home or on the Continent than in England. So it must be society, and here one's wonder deepens!

When I hear friends just back from a stay over there enlarging on the charms of "country life," or a London "season," I look attentively to see if they are in earnest, so incomparably dull have I always found English house parties or town entertainments. At least that side of society which the climbing stranger mostly affects. Other circles are charming, if a bit slow, and the "Bohemia" and semi-Bohemia of London have a delicate flavor of their own.

County society, that ideal life so attractive to American readers of British novels, is, taken on the whole, the most insipid existence conceivable. The women lack the sparkle and charm of ours; the men, who are out all day shooting or hunting according to the season, get back so fagged that if they do not actually drop asleep at the dinner-table, they will nap immediately after, brightening only when the ladies have retired, when, with evening dress changed for comfortable smoking suits, the hunters congregate in the billiard-room for cigars and brandy and seltzer.

A particularly agreeable American woman, whose husband insists on going every winter to Melton-Mowbray for the hunting, was describing the other day the life there among the women, and expressing her wonder that those who did not hunt could refrain from blowing out their brains, so awful was the dulness and monotony! She had ended by not dining out at all, having discovered that the conversation never by any chance deviated far from the knees of the horses and the height of the hedges!

Which reminds one of Thackeray relating how he had longed to know what women talked about when they were alone after dinner, imagining it to be on mysterious and thrilling subjects, until one evening he overheard such a conversation and found it turned entirely on children and ailments! As regards wit, the English are like the Oriental potentate who at a ball in Europe expressed his astonishment that the guests took the trouble to dance and get themselves hot and dishevelled, explaining that in the East he paid people to do that for him. In England "amusers" are invited expressly to be funny; anything uttered by one of these delightful individuals is sure to be received with much laughter. It is so simple that way! One is prepared and knows when to laugh. Whereas amateur wit is confusing. When an American I knew, turning over the books on a drawing-room table and finding Hare's Walks in London, in two volumes, said, "So you part your hair in the middle over here," the remark was received in silence, and with looks of polite surprise.

It is not necessary, however, to accumulate proofs that this much described society is less intelligent than our own. Their authors have acknowledged it, and well they may. For from Scott and Dickens down to Hall Caine, American appreciation has gone far toward establishing the reputation of English writers at home.

In spite of lack of humor and a thousand other defects which ought to make English swelldom antagonistic to our countrymen, the fact remains that "smart" London tempts a certain number of Americans and has become a promised land, toward which they turn longing eyes. You will always find a few of these votaries over there in the "season," struggling bravely up the social current, making acquaintances, spending money at charity sales, giving dinners and fetes, taking houses at Ascot and filling them with their new friends' friends. With more or less success as the new-comers have been able to return satisfactory answers to the three primary questions.

What Americans are these, who force us to blush for them infinitely more than for the unlettered tourists trotting conscientiously around the country, doing the sights and asking for soda-water and buckwheat cakes at the hotels!

Any one who has been an observer of the genus "Climber" at home, and wondered at their way and courage, will recognize these ambitious souls abroad; five minutes' conversation is enough. It is never about a place that they talk, but of the people they know. London to them is not the city of Dickens. It is a place where one may meet the Prince of Wales and perhaps obtain an entrance into his set.

One description will cover most climbers. They are, as a rule, people who start humbly in some small city, then when fortune comes, push on to New York and Newport, where they carry all before them and make their houses centres and themselves powers. Next comes the discovery that the circle into which they have forced their way is not nearly as attractive as it appeared from a distance. Consequently that vague disappointment is felt which most of us experience on attaining a long desired goal - the unsatisfactoriness of success! Much the same sensation as caused poor Du Maurier to answer, when asked shortly before his death why he looked so glum, "I'm soured by success!"

So true is this of all human nature that the following recipe might be given for the attainment of perfect happiness: "Begin far down in any walk of life. Rise by your efforts higher each year, and then be careful to die before discovering that there is nothing at the top. The excitement of the struggle - 'the rapture of the chase' - are greater joys than achievement."

Our ambitious friends naturally ignore this bit of philosophy. When it is discovered that the "world" at home has given but an unsatisfactory return for cash and conniving, it occurs to them that the fault lies in the circle, and they assume that their particular talents require a larger field. Having conquered all in sight, these social Alexanders pine for a new world, which generally turns out to be the "Old," so a crossing is made, and the "Conquest of England" begun with all the enthusiasm and push employed on starting out from the little native city twenty years before.

It is in Victoria's realm that foemen worthy of their steel await the conquerors. Home society was a too easy prey, opening its doors and laying down its arms at the first summons. In England the new-comers find that their little game has been played before; and, well, what they imagined was a discovery proves to be a long-studied science with "donnant! donnant!" as its fundamental law. Wily opponents with trump cards in their hands and a profound knowledge of "Hoyle" smilingly offer them seats. Having acquired in a home game a knowledge of "bluff," our friends plunge with delight into the fray, only to find English society so formed that, climb they never so wisely, the top can never be reached. Work as hard as they may, succeed even beyond their fondest hopes, there will always remain circles above, toward which to yearn - people who will refuse to know them, houses they will never be invited to enter. Think of the charm, the attraction such a civilization must have for the real born climber, and you, my reader, will understand why certain of our compatriots enjoy living in England, and why when once the intoxicating draught (supplied to the ambitious on the other side) has been tasted, all home concoctions prove insipid.

CHAPTER 10

CALVE AT CABRIERES

While I was making a "cure" last year at Lamalou, an obscure Spa in the Cevennes Mountains, Madame Calve, to whom I had expressed a desire to see her picturesque home, telegraphed an invitation to pass the day with her, naming the train she could meet, which would allow for the long drive to her chateau before luncheon. It is needless to say the invitation was accepted. As my train drew up at the little station, Madame Calve, in her trap, was the first person I saw, and no time was lost in getting en route.

During the hour passed on the poplar-bordered road that leads straight and white across the country I had time to appreciate the transformation in the woman at my side. Was this gray-clad, nunlike figure the passionate, sensuous Carmen of Bizet's masterpiece? Could that calm, pale face, crossed by innumerable lines of suffering, as a spider's web lies on a flower, blaze and pant with Sappho's guilty love?

Something of these thoughts must have appeared on my face, for turning with a smile, she asked, "You find me changed? It's the air of my village. Here I'm myself. Everywhere else I'm different. On the stage I am any part I may be playing, but am never really happy away from my hill there." As she spoke, a sun-baked hamlet came in sight, huddled around the base of two tall towers that rose cool and gray in the noonday heat.

"All that wing," she added, "is arranged for the convalescent girls whom I have sent down to me from the Paris hospitals for a cure of fresh air and simple food. Six years ago, just after I had bought this place, a series of operations became necessary which left me prostrated and anaemic. No tonics were of benefit. I grew weaker day by day, until the doctors began to despair of my life. Finally, at the advice of an old woman here who passes for being something of a curer, I tried the experiment or lying five or six hours a day motionless in the sunlight. It wasn't long before I felt life creeping back to my poor feeble body. The hot sun of our magic south was a more subtle tonic than any drug. When the cure was complete, I made up my mind that each summer the same chance should be offered to as many of my suffering sisters as this old place could be made to accommodate."

The bells on the shaggy Tarbes ponies she was driving along the Languedoc road drew, on nearing her residence, a number of peasant children from their play.

As the ruddy urchins ran shouting around our carriage wheels and scrambled in the dust for the sous we threw them, my hostess pointed laughing to a scrubby little girl with tomato-colored cheeks and tousled dark hair, remarking, "I looked like that twenty years ago and performed just those antics on this very road. No punishment would keep me off the highway. Those pennies, if I'm not mistaken, will all be spent at the village pastry cook's within an hour."

This was said with such a tender glance at the children that one realized the great artist was at home here, surrounded by the people she loved and understood. True to the "homing" instinct of the French peasant, Madame Calve, when fortune came to her, bought and partially restored the rambling chateau which at sunset casts its shadow across the village of her birth. Since that day every moment of freedom from professional labor and every penny of her large income are spent at Cabrieres, building, planning, even farming, when her health permits.

"I think," she continued, as we approached the chateau, "that the happiest day of my life - and I have, as you know, passed some hours worth living, both on and off the stage - was when, that wing completed, a Paris train brought the first occupants for my twenty little bedrooms; no words can tell the delight it gives me now to see the color coming back to my patients' pale lips and hear them laughing and singing about the place. As I am always short of funds, the idea of abandoning this work is the only fear the future holds for me."

With the vivacity peculiar to her character, my companion then whipped up her cobs and turned the conversation into gayer channels. Five minutes later we clattered over a drawbridge and drew up in a roomy courtyard, half blinding sunlight and half blue shadow, where a score of girls were occupied with books and sewing.

The luncheon bell was ringing as we ascended the terrace steps. After a hurried five minutes for brushing and washing, we took our places at a long table set in the cool stone hall, guests stopping in the chateau occupying one end around the chatelaine, the convalescents filling the other seats.

Those who have only seen the capricious diva on the stage or in Parisian salons can form little idea of the proprietress of Cabrieres. No shade of coquetry blurs the clear picture of her home life. The capped and saboted peasant women who waited on us were not more simple in their ways. Several times during the meal she left her seat to inquire after the comfort of some invalid girl or inspect the cooking in the adjacent kitchen. These wanderings were not, however, allowed to disturb the conversation, which flowed on after the mellow French fashion, enlivened by much wit and gay badinage. One of our hostess's anecdotes at her own expense was especially amusing.

"When in Venice," she told us, "most prima donnas are carried to and from the opera in sedan chairs to avoid the risk of colds from the draughty gondolas. The last night of my initial season there, I was informed, as the curtain fell, that a number of Venetian nobles were planning to carry me in triumph to the hotel. When I descended from my dressing-room the courtyard of the theatre was filled with men in dress clothes, bearing lanterns, who caught up the chair as soon as I was seated and carried it noisily across the city to the hotel. Much moved by this unusual honor, I mounted to the balcony of my room, from which elevation I bowed my thanks, and threw all the flowers at hand to my escort.

"Next morning the hotel proprietor appeared with my coffee, and after hesitating a moment, remarked: 'Well, we made a success of it last night. It has been telegraphed to all the capitals of Europe! I hope you will not think a thousand francs too much, considering the advertisement!' In blank amazement, I asked what he meant. 'I mean the triumphal progress,' he answered. 'I thought you understood! We always organize one for the "stars" who visit Venice. The men who carried your chair last night were the waiters from the hotels. We hire them on account of their dress clothes'! Think of the disillusion," added Calve, laughing, "and my disgust, when I thought of myself naively throwing kisses and flowers to a group of Swiss garcons at fifteen francs a head. There was nothing to do, however, but pay the bill and swallow my chagrin!"

How many pretty women do you suppose would tell such a joke upon themselves? Another story she told us is characteristic of her peasant neighbors.

"When I came back here after my first season in St. Petersburg and London the cure requested me to sing at our local fete. I gladly consented, and, standing by his side on the steps of the Mairie, gave the great aria from the Huguenots in my best manner. To my astonishment the performance was received in complete silence. 'Poor Calve,' I heard an old friend of my mother's murmur. 'Her voice used to be so nice, and now it's all gone!' Taking in the situation at a glance, I threw my voice well up into my nose and started off on a well-known provincial song, in the shrill falsetto of our peasant women. The effect was instantaneous! Long before the end the performance was drowned in thunders of applause. Which proves that to be popular a singer must adapt herself to her audience."

Luncheon over, we repaired for cigarettes and coffee to an upper room, where Calve was giving Dagnan-Bouveret some sittings for a portrait, and lingered there until four o'clock, when our hostess left us for her siesta, and a "break" took those who cared for the excursion across the valley to inspect the ruins of a Roman bath. A late dinner brought us together again in a small dining room, the convalescents having eaten their simple meal and disappeared an hour before. During this time, another transformation had taken place in our mercurial hostess! It was the Calve of Paris, Calve the witch, Calve the capiteuse, who presided at the dainty, flower-decked table and led the laughing conversation.

A few notes struck on a guitar by one of the party, as we sat an hour later on the moonlit terrace, were enough to start off the versatile artist, who was in her gayest humor. She sang us stray bits of opera, alternating her music with scenes burlesqued from recent plays. No one escaped her inimitable mimicry, not even the "divine Sarah," Calve giving us an unpayable impersonation of the elderly tragedienne as Lorenzaccio, the boy hero of Alfred de Musset's drama. Burlesquing led to her dancing some Spanish steps with an abandon never attempted on the stage! Which in turn gave place to an imitation of an American whistling an air from Carmen, and some "coon songs" she had picked up during her stay at New York. They, again, were succeeded by a superb rendering of the imprecation from Racine's Camille, which made her audience realize that in gaining a soprano the world has lost, perhaps, its greatest tragedienne.

At eleven o'clock the clatter of hoofs in the court

warned us that the pleasant evening had come to an end. A journalist en route for Paris was soon installed with me in the little omnibus that was to take us to the station, Calve herself lighting our cigars and providing the wraps that were to keep out the cool night air.

As we passed under the low archway of the entrance amid a clamor of "adieu" and "au revoir," the young Frenchman at my side pointed up to a row of closed windows overhead. "Isn't it a lesson," he said, "for all of us, to think of the occupants of those little rooms, whom the generosity and care of that gracious artist are leaning by such pleasant paths back to health and courage for their toilsome lives?"

CHAPTER 11

A CRY FOR FRESH AIR

"Once upon a time," reads the familiar nursery tale, while the fairies, invited by a king and queen to the christening of their daughter, were showering good gifts on the baby princess, a disgruntled old witch, whom no one had thought of asking to the ceremony, appeared uninvited on the scene and revenged herself by decreeing that the presents of the good fairies, instead of proving beneficial, should bring only trouble and embarrassment to the royal infant.

A telling analogy might be drawn between that unhappy princess over whose fate so many youthful tears have been shed, and the condition of our invention-ridden country; for we see every day how the good gifts of those nineteenth century fairies, Science and Industry, instead of proving blessings to mankind, are being turned by ignorance and stupidity into veritable afflictions.

If a prophetic gentleman had told Louis Fourteenth's shivering courtiers - whom an iron etiquette forced on winter mornings into the (appropriately named) Galerie des Glaces, stamping their silk-clad feet and blowing on their blue fingers, until the king should appear - that within a century and a half one simple discovery would enable all classes of people to keep their shops and dwellings at a summer temperature through the severest winters, the half-frozen nobles would have flouted the suggestion as an "iridescent dream," a sort of too-good-to-be-true prophecy.

What was to those noblemen an unheard-of luxury has become within the last decade one of the primary necessities of our life.

The question arises now: Are we gainers by the change? Has the indiscriminate use of heat been of advantage, either mentally or physically, to the nation?

The incubus of caloric that sits on our gasping country is particularly painful at this season, when nature undertakes to do her own heating.

In other less-favored lands, the first spring days, the exquisite awakening of the world after a long winter, bring to the inhabitants a sensation of joy and renewed vitality. We, however, have discounted that enjoyment. Delicate gradations of temperature are lost on people who have been stewing for six months in a mixture of steam and twice-breathed air.

What pleasure can an early April day afford the man who has slept in an overheated flat and is hurrying to an office where eighty degrees is the average all the year round? Or the pale shop-girl, who complains if a breath of morning air strays into the suburban train where she is seated?

As people who habitually use such "relishes" as Chutney and Worcestershire are incapable of appreciating delicately prepared food, so the "soft" mortals who have accustomed themselves to a perpetual August are insensible to fine shadings of temperature.

The other day I went with a friend to inspect some rooms he had been decorating in one of our public schools. The morning had been frosty, but by eleven o'clock the sun warmed the air uncomfortably. On entering the school we were met by a blast of heated air that was positively staggering. In the recitation rooms, where, as in all New York schoolrooms, the children were packed like dominoes in a box, the temperature could not have been under eighty-five.

The pale, spectacled spinster in charge, to whom we complained of this, was astonished and offended at what she considered our interference, and answered that "the children liked it warm," as for herself she "had a cold and could not think of opening a window." If the rooms were too warm it was the janitor's fault, and he had gone out!

Twelve o'clock struck before we had finished our tour of inspection. It is to be doubted if anywhere else in the world could there be found such a procession of pasty-faced, dull-eyed youngsters as trooped past us down the stairs. Their appearance was the natural result of compelling children dressed for winter weather to sit many hours each day in hothouses, more suited to tropical plants than to growing human beings.

A gentleman with us remarked with a sigh, "I have been in almost every school in the city and find the same condition everywhere. It is terrible, but there doesn't seem to be any remedy for it." The taste for living in a red-hot atmosphere is growing on our people; even public vehicles have to be heated now to please the patrons.

When tiresome old Benjamin Franklin made stoves popular he struck a terrible blow at the health of his compatriots; the introduction of steam heat and consequent suppression of all health-giving ventilation did the rest; the rosy cheeks of American children went up the chimney with the last whiff of wood smoke, and have never returned. Much of our home life followed; no family can be expected to gather in cheerful converse around a "radiator."

How can this horror of fresh air among us be explained? If people really enjoy living in overheated rooms with little or no ventilation, why is it that we hear so much complaining, when during the summer months the thermometer runs up into the familiar nineties? Why are children hurried out of town, and why do wives consider it a necessity to desert their husbands?

It's rather inconsistent, to say the least, for not one of those deserters but would "kick" if the theatre or church they attend fell below that temperature in December.

It is impossible to go into our banks and offices and not realize that the air has been breathed again and again, heated and cooled, but never changed, - doors and windows fit too tightly for that.

The pallor and dazed expression of the employees tell the same tale. I spoke to a youth the other day in an office about his appearance and asked if he was ill. "Yes," he answered, "I have had a succession of colds all winter. You see, my desk here is next to the radiator, so I am in a perpetual perspiration and catch cold as soon as I go out. Last winter I passed three months in a farmhouse, where the water froze in my room at night, and we had to wear overcoats to our meals. Yet I never had a cold there, and gained in weight and strength."

Twenty years ago no "palatial private residence" was considered complete unless there was a stationary washstand (forming a direct connection with the sewer) in each bedroom. We looked pityingly on foreigners who did not enjoy these advantages, until one day we realized that the latter were in the right, and straightway stationary washstands disappeared.

How much time must pass and how many victims be sacrificed before we come to our senses on the great radiator question?

As a result of our population living in a furnace, it happens now that when you rebel on being forced to take an impromptu Turkish bath at a theatre, the usher answers your complaint with "It can't be as warm as you think, for a lady over there has just told me she felt chilly and asked for more heat!"

Another invention of the enemy is the "revolving door." By this ingenious contrivance the little fresh air that formerly crept into a building is now excluded. Which explains why on entering our larger hotels one is taken by the throat, as it were, by a sickening long-dead atmosphere - in which the souvenir of past meals and decaying flowers floats like a regret - such as explorers must find on opening an Egyptian tomb.

Absurd as it may seem, it has become a distinction to

have cool rooms. Alas, they are rare! Those blessed households where one has the delicious sensation of being chilly and can turn with pleasure toward crackling wood! The open fire has become, within the last decade, a test of refinement, almost a question of good breeding, forming a broad distinction between dainty households and vulgar ones, and marking the line which separates the homes of cultivated people from the parlors of those who care only for display.

A drawing-room filled with heat, the source of which remains invisible, is as characteristic of the parvenu as clanking chains on a harness or fine clothes worn in the street.

An open fire is the "eye" of a room, which can no more be attractive without it than the human face can be beautiful if it lacks the visual organs. The "gas fire" bears about the same relation to the real thing as a glass eye does to a natural one, and produces much the same sensation. Artificial eyes are painful necessities in some cases, and therefore cannot be condemned; but the household which gathers complacently around a "gas log" must have something radically wrong with it, and would be capable of worse offences against taste and hospitality.

There is a tombstone in a New England grave-yard the inscription on which reads: "I was well, I wanted to be better. Here I am."

As regards heating of our houses, it's to be feared that we have gone much the same road as the unfortunate New Englander. I don't mean to imply that he is now suffering from too much heat, but we, as a nation, certainly are.

Janitors and parlor-car conductors have replaced the wicked fairies of other days, but are apparently animated by their malignant spirit, and employ their hours of brief authority as cruelly. No witch dancing around her boiling cauldron was ever more joyful than the fireman of a modern hotel, as he gleefully turns more and more steam upon his helpless victims. Long acquaintance with that gentleman has convinced me that he cannot plead ignorance as an excuse for falling into these excesses. It is pure, unadulterated perversity, else why should he invariably choose the mildest mornings to show what his engines can do?

Many explanations have been offered for this love of a high temperature by our compatriots. Perhaps the true one has not yet been found. Is it not possible that what appears to be folly and almost criminal negligence of the rules of health, may be, after all, only a commendable ambition to renew the exploits of those biblical heroes, Shadrach, Meshach, and Abednego?

CHAPTER 12

THE PARIS OF OUR GRANDPARENTS

We are apt to fall into the error of assuming that only American cities have displaced their centres and changed their appearance during the last half-century.

The "oldest inhabitant," with his twice-told tales of transformations and changes, is to a certain extent responsible for this; by contrast, we imagine that the capitals of Europe have always been just as we see them. So strong is this impression that it requires a serious effort of the imagination to reconstruct the Paris that our grandparents knew and admired, few as the years are that separate their day from ours.

It is, for instance, difficult to conceive of a Paris that ended at the rue Royale, with only waste land and market gardens beyond the Madeleine, where to-day so many avenues open their stately perspectives; yet such was the case! The few fine residences that existed beyond that point faced the Faubourg Saint-Honore, with gardens running back to an unkempt open country called the Champs Elysees, where an unfinished Arc de Triomphe stood alone in a wilderness that no one ever dreamed of traversing.

The fashionable ladies of that time drove in the

afternoon along the boulevards from the Madeleine to the Chateau d'Eau, and stopped their ponderous yellow barouches at Tortoni's, where ices were served to them in their carriages, while they chatted with immaculate dandies in skin-tight nankeen unmentionables, blue swallow-tailed coats, and furry 'beaver" hats.

While looking over some books in the company of an old lady who from time to time opens her store of treasures and recalls her remote youth at my request, and whose spirituel and graphic language gives to her souvenirs the air of being stray chapters from some old-fashioned romance, I received a vivid impression of how the French capital must have looked fifty years ago.

Emptying in her company a chest of books that had not seen the light for several decades, we came across a "Panorama of the Boulevards," dated 1845, which proved when unfolded to be a colored lithograph, a couple of yards long by five or six inches high, representing the line of boulevards from the Madeleine to the Place de la Bastille. Each house, almost each tree, was faithfully depicted, together with the crowds on the sidewalks and the carriages in the street. The whole scene was as different from the effect made by that thoroughfare to-day as though five hundred and not fifty years had elapsed since the little book was printed. The picture breathed an atmosphere of calm and nameless quaintness that one finds now only in old provincial cities which have escaped the ravages of improvement.

My companion sat with the book unfolded before her, in a smiling trance. Her mind had turned back to the far-away days when she first trod those streets a bride,

with all the pleasures and few of the cares of life to
think about.

I watched her in silence (it seemed a sacrilege to break
in on such a train of thought), until gradually her eyes
lost their far-away expression, and, turning to me with
a smile, she exclaimed: "How we ever had the courage
to appear in the street dressed as we were is a mystery!
Do you see that carriage?" pointing in the print to a
high-swung family vehicle with a powdered coachman
on the box, and two sky-blue lackeys standing behind.
"I can remember, as if it were yesterday, going to drive
with Lady B-, the British ambassadress, in just such a
conveyance. She drove four horses with feathers on
their heads, when she used to come to Meurice's for
me. I blush when I think that my frock was so scant
that I had to raise the skirt almost to my knees in order
to get into her carriage.

"Why we didn't all die of pneumonia is another marvel,
for we wore low-necked dresses and the thinnest of
slippers in the street, our heads being about the only
part that was completely covered. I was particularly
proud of a turban surmounted with a bird of paradise,
but Lady B - affected poke bonnets, then just coming
into fashion, so large and so deep that when one looked
at her from the side nothing was visible except two
curls, 'as damp and as black as leeches.' In other ways
our toilets were absurdly unsuited for every-day wear;
we wore light scarves over our necks, and rarely used
furlined pelisses."

Returning to an examination of the panorama, my
companion pointed out to me that there was no break
in the boulevards, where the opera-house, with its
seven radiating avenues, now stands, but a long line of

Hotels, dozing behind high walls, and quaint two-storied buildings that undoubtedly dated from the razing of the city wall and the opening of the new thoroughfare under Louis XV.

A little farther on was the world-famous Maison Doree, where one almost expected to see Alfred de Musset and le docteur Veron dining with Dumas and Eugene Sue.

"What in the name of goodness is that?" I exclaimed, pointing to a couple of black and yellow monstrosities on wheels, which looked like three carriages joined together with a "buggy" added on in front.

"That's the diligence just arrived from Calais; it has been two days en route, the passengers sleeping as best they could, side by side, and escaping from their confinement only when horses were changed or while stopping for meals. That high two-wheeled trap with the little 'tiger' standing up behind is a tilbury. We used to see the Count d'Orsay driving one like that almost every day. He wore butter-colored gloves, and the skirts of his coat were pleated full all around, and stood out like a ballet girl's. It is a pity they have not included Louis Philippe and his family jogging off to Neuilly in the court 'carryall,' - the 'Citizen King,' with his blue umbrella between his knees, trying to look like an honest bourgeois, and failing even in that attempt to please the Parisians.

"We were in Paris in '48; from my window at Meurice's I saw poor old Juste Milieu read his abdication from the historic middle balcony of the Tuileries, and half an hour later we perceived the Duchesse d'Orleans leave the Tuileries on foot, leading her two sons by the hand, and walk through the gardens and across the Place de la Concorde to the Corps Legislatif, in a last attempt to save the crown for her son. Futile effort! That evening the 'Citizen King' was hurried through those same gardens and into a passing cab, en route for a life exile.

"Our balcony at Meurice's was a fine point of observation from which to watch a revolution. With an opera-glass we could see the mob surging to the sack of the palace, the priceless furniture and bric-a-brac flung into the street, court dresses waved on pikes from the tall windows, and finally the throne brought out, and carried off to be burned. There was no keeping the men of our party in after that. They rushed off to have a nearer glimpse of the fighting, and we saw no more of them until daybreak the following morning when, just as we were preparing to send for the police, two dilapidated, ragged, black-faced mortals appeared, in whom we barely recognized our husbands. They had been impressed into service and passed their night building barricades. My better half, however, had succeeded in snatching a handful of the gold fringe from the throne as it was carried by, an act of prowess that repaid him for all his troubles and fatigue.

"I passed the greater part of forty-eight hours on our balcony, watching the mob marching by, singing La Marseillaise, and camping at night in the streets. It was all I could do to tear myself away from the window long enough to eat and write in my journal.

"There was no Avenue de l'Opera then. The trip from the boulevards to the Palais-Royal had to be made by a long detour across the Place Vendome (where, by the bye, a cattle market was held) or through a labyrinth of narrow, bad-smelling little streets, where strangers easily lost their way. Next to the boulevards, the Palais-Royal was the centre of the elegant and dissipated life in the capital. It was there we met of an afternoon to drink chocolate at the 'Rotonde,' or to dine at 'Les Trois Freres Provencaux,' and let our husbands have a try at the gambling tables in the Passage d'Orleans.

"No one thought of buying jewelry anywhere else. It was from the windows of its shops that the fashions started on their way around the world. When Victoria as a bride was visiting Louis Philippe, she was so fascinated by the aspect of the place that the gallant French king ordered a miniature copy of the scene, made in papier-mache, as a present for his guest, a sort of gigantic dolls' house in which not only the palace and its long colonnades were reproduced, but every tiny shop and the myriad articles for sale were copied with Chinese fidelity. Unfortunately the pear-headed old king became England's uninvited guest before this clumsy toy was finished, so it never crossed the Channel, but can be seen to-day by any one curious enough to examine it, in the Musee Carnavalet.

"Few of us realize that the Paris of Charles X. and Louis Philippe would seem to us now a small, ill-paved, and worse-lighted provincial town, with few theatres or hotels, communicating with the outer world only by means of a horse-drawn 'post,' and practically farther from London than Constantinople is to-day. One feels this isolation in the literature of the time; brilliant as the epoch was, the horizon of its writers was bounded by the boulevards and the Faubourg Saint-Germain."

Dumas says laughingly, in a letter to a friend: "I have never ventured into the unexplored country beyond the Bastille, but am convinced that it shelters wild animals and savages." The wit and brains of the period were concentrated into a small space. Money-making had no more part in the programme of a writer then than an introduction into "society." Catering to a foreign market and snobbishness were undreamed-of degradations. Paris had not yet been turned into the Foire du Monde that she has since become, with whole quarters given over to the use of foreigners, - theatres, restaurants, and hotels created only for the use of a polyglot population that could give lessons to the people around Babel's famous "tower."

CHAPTER 13

SOME AMERICAN HUSBANDS

Until the beginning of this century men played the beau role in life's comedy. As in the rest of the animal world, our males were the brilliant members of the community, flaunting their gaudy plumage at home and abroad, while the women-folk remained in seclusion, tending their children, directing the servants, or ministering to their lords' comfort.

In those happy days the husband ruled supreme at his own fireside, receiving the homage of the family, who bent to his will and obeyed his orders.

During the last century, however, the "part" of better half has become less and less attractive in America, one prerogative after another having been whisked away by enterprising wives. Modern Delilahs have yearly snipped off more and more of Samson's luxuriant curls, and added those ornaments to their own coiffures, until in the majority of families the husband finds himself reduced to a state of bondage compared with which the biblical hero enjoyed a pampered idleness. Times have indeed changed in America since the native chief sat in dignified repose bedizened with all the finery at hand, while the ladies of the family waited tremblingly upon him. To-day it is the American husband who turns the grindstone all the year round, and it is his pretty tyrant who enjoys the elegant leisure that a century ago was considered a masculine luxury.

To America must be given the credit of having produced the model husband, a new species, as it were, of the genus homo.

In no role does a compatriot appear to such advantage as in that of Benedict. As a boy he is often too advanced for his years or his information; in youth he is conspicuous neither for his culture nor his unselfishness. But once in matrimonial harness this untrained animal becomes bridle-wise with surprising rapidity, and will for the rest of life go through his paces, waltzing, kneeing, and saluting with hardly a touch of the whip. Whether this is the result of superior horse-womanship on the part of American wives or a trait peculiar to sons of "Uncle Sam," is hard to say, but the fact is self-evident to any observer that our fair equestrians rarely meet with a rebellious mount.

Any one who has studied marital ways in other lands will realize that in no country have the men effaced themselves so gracefully as with us. In this respect no foreign production can compare for a moment with the domestic article. In English, French, and German families the husband is still all-powerful. The house is mounted, guests are asked, and the year planned out to suit his occupations and pleasure. Here papa is rarely consulted until such matters have been decided upon by the ladies, when the head of the house is called in to sign the checks.

I have had occasion more than once to bewail the

shortcomings of the American man, and so take pleasure in pointing out the modesty and good temper with which he fills this role. He is trained from the beginning to give all and expect nothing in return, an American girl rarely bringing any dot to her husband, no matter how wealthy her family may be. If, as occasionally happens, an income is allowed a bride by her parents, she expects to spend it on her toilets or pleasures. This condition of the matrimonial market exists in no other country; even in England, where mariages de convenance are rare, "settlements" form an inevitable prelude to conjugal bliss.

The fact that she contributes little or nothing to the common income in no way embarrasses an American wife; her pretensions are usually in an inverse proportion to her personal means. A man I knew some years ago deliberately chose his bride from an impecunious family (in the hope that her simple surroundings had inculcated homely taste), and announced to an incredulous circle of friends, at his last bachelor dinner, that he intended, in future, to pass his evenings at his fireside, between his book and his pretty spouse. Poor, innocent, confiding mortal! The wife quickly became a belle of the fastest set in town. Having had more than she wanted of firesides and quiet evenings before her marriage, her idea was to go about as much as possible, and, when not so occupied, to fill her house with company. It may be laid down as a maxim in this connection that a man marries to obtain a home, and a girl to get away from one; hence disappointment on both sides.

The couple in question have in all probability not passed an evening alone since they were married, the lady rarely stopping in the round of her gayeties until she collapses from fatigue. Their home is typical of their life, which itself can be taken as a good example of the existence that most of our "smart" people lead. The ground floor and the first floor are given up to entertaining. The second is occupied by the spacious sitting, bath, and sleeping rooms of the lady. A ten-by-twelve chamber suffices for my lord, and the only den he can rightly call his own is a small room near the front door, about as private as the sidewalk, which is turned into a cloak-room whenever the couple receive, making it impossible to keep books or papers of value there, or even to use it as a smoking-room after dinner, so his men guests sit around the dismantled dining-table while the ladies are enjoying a suite of parlors above.

At first the idea of such an unequal division of the house shocks our sense of justice, until we reflect that the American husband is not expected to remain at home. That's not his place! If he is not down town making money, fashion dictates that he must be at some club-house playing a game. A man who should remain at home, and read or chat with the ladies of his family, would be considered a bore and unmanly. There seems to be no place in an American house for its head. More than once when the friend I have referred to has asked me, at the club, to dine informally with him, we have found, on arriving, that Madame, having an evening off, had gone to bed and forgotten to order any dinner, so we were obliged to return to the club for our meal. When, however, his wife is in good health, she expects her weary husband to accompany her to dinner, opera, or ball, night after night, oblivious of the work the morrow holds in store for him.

In one family I know, paterfamilias goes by the name

of the "purse." The more one sees of American households the more appropriate that name appears. Everything is expected of the husband, and he is accorded no definite place in return. He leaves the house at 8.30. When he returns, at five, if his wife is entertaining a man at tea, it would be considered the height of indelicacy for him to intrude upon them, for his arrival would cast a chill on the conversation. When a couple dine out, the husband is always la bete noire of the hostess, no woman wanting to sit next to a married man, if she can help it.

The few Benedicts who have had the courage to break away from these conditions and amuse themselves with yachts, salmon rivers, or "grass-bachelor" trips to Europe, while secretly admired by the women, are frowned upon in society as dangerous examples, likely to sow the seeds of discontent among their comrades; although it is the commonest thing in the world for an American wife to take the children and go abroad on a tour.

Imagine a German or Italian wife announcing to her spouse that she had decided to run over to England for a year with her children, that they might learn English. The mind recoils in horror from the idea of the catastrophe that would ensue.

Glance around a ball-room, a dinner party, or the opera, if you have any doubts as to the unselfishness of our married men. How many of them do you suppose are present for their own pleasure? The owner of an opera box rarely retains a seat in his expensive quarters. You generally find him idling in the lobbies looking at his watch, or repairing to a neighboring concert hall to pass the weary hours. At a ball it is even worse. One wonders why card-rooms are not provided at large balls (as is the custom abroad), where the bored husbands might find a little solace over "bridge," instead of yawning in the coat-room or making desperate signs to their wives from the doorway, - signals of distress, by the bye, that rarely produce any effect.

It is the rebellious husband who is admired and courted, however. A curious trait of human nature compels admiration for whatever is harmful, and forces us, in spite of our better judgment, to depreciate the useful and beneficent. The coats-of-arms of all countries are crowded with eagles and lions, that never yet did any good, living or dead; orators enlarge on the fine qualities of these birds and beasts, and hold them up as models, while using as terms of reproach the name of the goose or the cow, creatures that minister in a hundred ways to our wants. Such a spirit has brought helpful, productive "better halves" to the humble place they now occupy in the eyes of our people.

As long as men passed their time in fighting and carousing they were heroes; as soon as they became patient bread-winners all the romance evaporated from their atmosphere. The Jewish Hercules had his revenge in the end and made things disagreeable for his tormentors. So far, however, there are no signs of a revolt among the shorn lambs in this country. They patiently bend their necks to the collar - the kindest, most loving and devoted helpmates that ever plodded under the matrimonial yoke.

When in the East, one watches with admiration the part a donkey plays in the economy of those primitive lands. All the work is reserved for that industrious animal, and little play falls to his share. The camel is always bad-tempered, and when overladen lies down, refusing to move until relieved of its burden. The Turk is lazy and selfish, the native women pass their time in chattering and giggling, the children play and squabble, the ubiquitous dog sleeps in the sun; but from daybreak to midnight the little mouse-colored donkeys toil unceasingly. All burdens too bulky or too cumbersome for man are put on his back; the provender which horses and camels have refused becomes his portion; he is the first to begin the day's labor, and the last to turn in. It is impossible to live long in the Orient or the south of France without becoming attached to those gentle, willing animals. The role which honest "Bourico" fills so well abroad is played on this side of the Atlantic by the American husband.

I mean no disrespect to my married compatriots; on the contrary, I admire them as I do all docile, unselfish beings. It is well for our women, however, that their lords, like the little Oriental donkeys, ignore their strength, and are content to toil on to the end of their days, expecting neither praise nor thanks in return.

CHAPTER 14

"CAROLUS"

In the early seventies a group of students - dissatisfied with the cut-and-dried instruction of the Paris art school and attracted by certain qualities of color and technique in the work of a young Frenchman from the city of Lille, who was just beginning to attract the attention of connoisseurs - went in a body to his studio with the request that he would oversee their work and direct their studies. The artist thus chosen was Carolus-Duran. Oddly enough, a majority of the youths who sought him out and made him their master were Americans.

The first modest workroom on the Boulevard Montparnasse was soon too small to hold the pupils who crowded under this newly raised banner, and a move was made to more commodious quarters near the master's private studio. Sargent, Dannat, Harrison, Beckwith, Hinckley, and many others whom it is needless to mention here, will - if these lines come under their notice - doubtless recall with a thrill of pleasure the roomy one-storied structure in the rue Notre-Dame des Champs where we established our atelier d'eleves, a self-supporting cooperative concern, each student contributing ten francs a month toward rent, fire, and models, "Carolus" - the name by which this master is universally known abroad - not only refusing all compensation, according to the immutable custom of French painters of distinction, but, as we discovered later, contributing too often from his own pocket to help out the massier at the end of a difficult season, or smooth the path of some improvident pupil.

Those were cloudless, enchanted days we passed in the tumbled down old atelier: an ardent springtime of life when the future beckons gayly and no doubts of success obscure the horizon. Our young master's enthusiasm fired his circle of pupils, who, as each succeeding year brought him increasing fame, revelled in a reflected glory with the generous admiration of youth, in which there is neither calculation nor shadow of envy.

A portrait of Madame de Portalais, exhibited about this time, drew all art-loving Paris around the new celebrity's canvas. Shortly after, the government purchased a painting (of our master's beautiful wife), now known as La Femme au Gant, for the Luxembourg Gallery.

It is difficult to overestimate the impetus that a master's successes impart to the progress of his pupils. My first studious year in Paris had been passed in the shadow of an elderly painter, who was comfortably dozing on the laurels of thirty years before. The change from that sleepy environment to the vivid enthusiasm and dash of Carolus-Duran's studio was like stepping out of a musty cloister into the warmth and movement of a market-place.

Here, be it said in passing, lies perhaps the secret of the dry rot that too often settles on our American art schools. We, for some unknown reason, do not take the work of native painters seriously, nor encourage them in proportion to their merit. In consequence they retain but a feeble hold upon their pupils.

Carolus, handsome, young, successful, courted, was an ideal leader for a band of ambitious, high-strung youths, repaying their devotion with an untiring interest and lifting clever and dull alike on the strong wings of his genius. His visits to the studio, on which his friend Henner often accompanied him, were frequent and prolonged; certain Tuesdays being especially appreciated by us, as they were set apart for his criticism of original compositions.

When our sketches (the subject for which had been given out in advance) were arranged, and we had seated ourselves in a big half-circle on the floor, Carolus would install himself on a tall stool, the one seat the studio boasted, and chat a propos of the works before him on composition, on classic art, on the theories of color and clair-obscur. Brilliant talks, inlaid with much wit and incisive criticism, the memory of which must linger in the minds of all who were fortunate enough to hear them. Nor was it to the studio alone that our master's interest followed us. He would drop in at the Louvre, when we were copying there, and after some pleasant words of advice and encouragement, lead us off for a stroll through the galleries, interrupted by stations before his favorite masterpieces.

So important has he always considered a constant study of Renaissance art that recently, when about to commence his Triumph of Bacchus, Carolus copied one of Rubens's larger canvases with all the naivete of a beginner.

An occasion soon presented itself for us to learn another side of our trade by working with our master on a ceiling ordered of him by the state for the Palace of the Luxembourg. The vast studios which the city of Paris provides on occasions of this kind, with a liberality that should make our home corporations reflect, are situated out beyond the Exhibition buildings, in a curious, unfrequented quarter, ignored alike by Parisians and tourists, where the city stores compromising statues and the valuable debris of her many revolutions. There, among throneless Napoleons and riderless bronze steeds, we toiled for over six months side by side with our master, on gigantic Apotheosis of Marie de Medicis, serving in turn as painter and painted, and leaving the imprint of our hands and the reflection of our faces scattered about the composition. Day after day, when work was over, we would hoist the big canvas by means of a system of ropes and pulleys, from a perpendicular to the horizontal position it was to occupy permanently, and then sit straining our necks and discussing the progress of the work until the tardy spring twilight warned us to depart.

The year 1877 brought Carolus-Duran the medaille d'honneur, a crowning recompense that set the atelier mad with delight. We immediately organized a great (but economical) banquet to commemorate the event, over which our master presided, with much modesty, considering the amount of incense we burned before him, and the speeches we made. One of our number even burst into some very bad French verses, asserting that the painters of the world in general fell back before him -

. . . epouvantes - Craignant egalement sa brosse et

son epee.

This allusion to his proficiency in fencing was considered particularly neat, and became the favorite song of the studio, to be howled in and out of season.

Curiously enough, there is always something in Carolus-Duran's attitude when at work which recalls the swordsman. With an enormous palette in one hand and a brush in the other, he has a way of planting himself in front of his sitter that is amusingly suggestive of a duel. His lithe body sways to and fro, his fine leonine face quivers with the intense study of his model; then with a sudden spring forward, a few rapid touches are dashed on the canvas (like home strokes in the enemy's weakest spot) with a precision of hand acquired only by long years of fencing.

An order to paint the king and queen of Portugal was the next step on the road to fame, another rung on the pleasant ladder of success. When this work was done the delighted sovereign presented the painter with the order of "Christ of Portugal," together with many other gifts, among which a caricature of the master at work, signed by his sitter, is not the least valued.

When the great schism occurred several years ago which rent the art world of France, Carolus-Duran was elected vice-president of the new school under Meissonier, to whose office he succeeded on that master's death; and now directs and presides over the yearly exhibition known as the Salon du Champ de Mars.

At his chateau near Paris or at Saint Raphael, on the Mediterranean, the master lives, like Leonardo of old, the existence of a grand seigneur, surrounded by his family, innumerable guests, and the horses and dogs he loves, - a group of which his ornate figure and expressive face form the natural centre. Each year he lives more away from the world, but no more inspiriting sight can be imagined than the welcome the president receives of a "varnishing" day, when he makes his entry surrounded by his pupils. The students cheer themselves hoarse, and the public climbs on everything that comes to hand to see him pass. It is hard to realize then that this is the same man who, not content with his youthful progress, retired into an Italian monastery that he might commune face to face with nature undisturbed.

The works of no other painter give me the same sensation of quivering vitality, except the Velasquez in the Madrid Gallery and, perhaps, Sargent at his best; and one feels all through the American painter's work the influence of his first and only master.

"Tout ce qui n'est pas indispensable est nuisible," a phrase which is often on Carolus-Duran's lips, may be taken as the keynote of his work, where one finds a noble simplicity of line and color scheme, an elimination of useless detail, a contempt for tricks to enforce an effect, and above all a comprehension and mastery of light, vitality, and texture - those three unities of the painter's art - that bring his canvases very near to those of his self-imposed Spanish master.

Those who know the French painter's more important works and his many splendid studies from the nude, feel it a pity that such masterpieces as the equestrian portrait of Mlle. Croisette, of the Comedie Francaise, the Reveil, the superb full length of Mme. Pelouse on the Terrace of Chenonceau, and the head of Gounod in the Luxembourg, could not be collected into one exhibition, that lovers of art here in America might realize for themselves how this master's works are of the class that typify a school and an epoch, and engrave their author's name among those destined to become household words in the mouths of future generations.

CHAPTER 15

THE GRAND OPERA FAD

Without being more curious than my neighbors, there are several social mysteries that I should like to fathom, among others, the real reasons that induce the different classes of people one sees at the opera to attend that form of entertainment.

A taste for the theatre is natural enough. It is also easy to understand why people who are fond of sport and animals enjoy races and dog shows. But the continued vogue of grand opera, and more especially of Wagner's long-drawn-out compositions, among our restless, unmusical compatriots, remains unexplained.

The sheeplike docility of our public is apparent in numberless ways; in none, however, more strikingly than in their choice of amusements. In business and religion, people occasionally think for themselves; in the selection of entertainments, never! but are apparently content to receive their opinions and prejudices ready-made from some unseen and omnipotent Areopagus.

The careful study of an opera audience from different parts of our auditorium has brought me to the conclusion that the public there may be loosely divided into three classes - leaving out reporters of fashionable intelligence, dressmakers in search of ideas, and the lady inhabitants of "Crank Alley" (as a certain corner of the orchestra is called), who sit in perpetual adoration before the elderly tenor.

First - but before venturing further on dangerously thin ice, it may be as well to suggest that this subject is not treated in absolute seriousness, and that all assertions must not be taken au pied de la lettre. First, then, and most important, come the stockholders, for without them the Metropolitan would close. The majority of these fortunate people and their guests look upon the opera as a social function, where one can meet one's friends and be seen, an entertaining antechamber in which to linger until it's time to "go on," her Box being to-day as necessary a part of a great lady's outfit as a country house or a ball-room.

Second are those who attend because it has become the correct thing to be seen at the opera. There is so much wealth in this city and so little opportunity for its display, so many people long to go about who are asked nowhere, that the opera has been seized upon as a centre in which to air rich apparel and elbow the "world." This list fills a large part of the closely packed parquet and first balcony.

Third, and last, come the lovers of music, who mostly inhabit greater altitudes.

The motive of the typical box-owner is simple. Her night at the opera is the excuse for a cosy little dinner, one woman friend (two would spoil the effect of the box) and four men, without counting the husband, who appears at dinner, but rarely goes further. The pleasant meal and the subsequent smoke are prolonged until 9 or 9.30, when the men are finally dragged murmuring from their cigars. If she has been fortunate and timed her arrival to correspond with an entr'acte, my lady is radiant. The lights are up, she can see who are present, and the public can inspect her toilet and jewels as she settles herself under the combined gaze of the house, and proceeds to hold an informal reception for the rest of the evening. The men she has brought with her quickly cede their places to callers, and wander yawning in the lobby or invade the neighboring boxes and add their voices to the general murmur.

Although there is much less talking than formerly, it is the toleration of this custom at all by the public that indicates (along with many other straws) that we are not a music-loving people. Audible conversation during a performance would not be allowed for a moment by a Continental audience. The little visiting that takes place in boxes abroad is done during the entr'actes, when people retire to the salons back of their loges to eat ices and chat. Here those little parlors are turned into cloak-rooms, and small talk goes on in many boxes during the entire performance. The joke or scandal of the day is discussed; strangers in town, or literary and artistic lights - "freaks," they are discriminatingly called - are pointed out, toilets passed in review, and those dreadful two hours passed which, for some undiscovered reason, must elapse between a dinner and a dance. If a favorite tenor is singing, and no one happens to be whispering nonsense over her shoulder, my lady may listen in a distrait way. It is not safe, however, to count on prolonged attention or ask her questions about the performance. She is apt to be a bit hazy as to who is singing, and with the exception of Faust and Carmen, has rudimentary ideas about plots.

Singers come and go, weep, swoon, or are killed, without interfering with her equanimity. She has, for instance, seen the Huguenots and the Rheingold dozens of times, but knows no more why Raoul is brought blindfolded to Chenonceaux, or what Wotan and Erda say to each other in their interminable scenes, than she does of the contents of the Vedas. For the matter of that, if three or four principal airs were suppressed from an opera and the scenery and costumes changed, many in that chattering circle would, I fear, not know what they were listening to.

Last winter, when Melba sang in Aida, disguised by dark hair and a brown skin, a lady near me vouchsafed the opinion that the "little black woman hadn't a bad voice;" a gentleman (to whom I remarked last week "that as Sembrich had sung Rosina in the Barber, it was rather a shock to see her appear as that lady's servant in the Mariage de Figaro") looked his blank amazement until it was explained to him that one of those operas was a continuation of the other. After a pause he remarked, "They are not by the same composer, anyway! Because the first's by Rossini, and the Mariage is by Bon Marche. I've been at his shop in Paris."

The presence of the second category - the would-be fashionable people - is not so easily accounted for. Their attendance can hardly be attributed to love of melody, as they are, if anything, a shade less musical than the box-dwellers, who, by the bye, seem to exercise an irresistible fascination, to judge by the trend of conversation and direction of glasses. Although an imposing and sufficiently attentive throng, it would be difficult to find a less discrimi-nating public than that which gathers nightly in the

Metropolitan parterre. One wonders how many of those people care for music and how many attend because it is expensive and "swell."

They will listen with the same bland contentment to either bad or good performances so long as a world-renowned artist (some one who is being paid a comfortable little fortune for the evening) is on the stage. The orchestra may be badly led (it often is); the singers may flat - or be out of voice; the performance may go all at sixes and sevens - there is never a murmur of dissent. Faults that would set an entire audience at Naples or Milan hissing are accepted herewith ignorant approval.

The unfortunate part of it is that this weakness of ours has become known. The singers feel they can give an American audience any slipshod performance. I have seen a favorite soprano shrug her shoulders as she entered her dressing-room and exclaim: "Mon Dieu! How I shuffled through that act! They'd have hooted me off the stage in Berlin, but here no one seems to care. Did you notice the baritone to-night? He wasn't on the key once during our duo. I cannot sing my best, try as I will, when I hear the public applauding good and bad alike!"

It is strange that our pleasure-loving rich people should have hit on the opera as a favorite haunt. We and the English are the only race who will attend performances in a foreign language which we don't understand. How can intelligent people who don't care for music go on, season after season, listening to operas, the plots of which they ignore, and which in their hearts they find dull?

Is it so very amusing to watch two middle-aged ladies nagging each other, at two o'clock in the morning, on a public square, as they do in Lohengrin? Do people find the lecture that Isolde's husband delivers to the guilty lovers entertaining? Does an opera produce any illusion on my neighbors? I wish it did on me! I see too plainly the paint on the singers' hot faces and the cords straining in their tired throats! I sit on certain nights in agony, fearing to see stout Romeo roll on the stage in apoplexy! The sopranos, too, have a way, when about to emit a roulade, that is more suggestive of a dentist's chair, and the attendant gargle, than of a love phrase.

When two celebrities combine in a final duo, facing the public and not each other, they give the impression of victims whom an unseen inquisitor is torturing. Each turn of his screw draws out a wilder cry. The orchestra (in the pay of the demon) does all it can to prevent their shrieks from reaching the public. The lovers in turn redouble their efforts; they are purple in the face and glistening with perspiration. Defeat, they know, is before them, for the orchestra has the greater staying power! The flutes bleat; the trombones grunt; the fiddles squeal; an epileptic leader cuts wildly into the air about him. When, finally, their strength exhausted, the breathless human beings, with one last ear-piercing note, give up the struggle and retire, the public, excited by the unequal contest, bursts into thunders of applause.

Why wouldn't it be a good idea, in order to avoid these painful exhibitions, to have an arrangement of screens, with the singing people behind and a company of young and attractive pantomimists going through the gestures and movements in front? Otherwise, how can the most imaginative natures lose themselves at an opera? Even when the singers are comely, there is always that eternal double row of stony-faced witnesses in full view, whom no crimes astonish and no misfortunes melt. It takes most of the poetry out of Faust's first words with Marguerite, to have that short interview interrupted by a line of old, weary women shouting, "Let us whirl in the waltz o'er the mount and the plain!" Or when Scotch Lucy appears in a smart tea-gown and is good enough to perform difficult exercises before a half-circle of Italian gentlemen in pantalets and ladies in court costumes, does she give any one the illusion of an abandoned wife dying of a broken heart alone in the Highlands? Broken heart, indeed! It's much more likely she'll die of a ruptured blood-vessel!

Philistines in matters musical, like myself, unfortunate mortals whom the sweetest sounds fail to enthrall when connected with no memory or idea, or when prolonged beyond a limited period, must approach the third group with hesitation and awe. That they are sincere, is evident. The rapt expressions of their faces, and their patience, bear testimony to this fact. For a long time I asked myself, "Where have I seen that intense, absorbed attitude before?" Suddenly one evening another scene rose in my memory.

Have you ever visited Tangiers? In the market-place of that city you will find the inhabitants crouched by hundreds around their native musicians. When we were there, one old duffer - the Wagner, doubtless, of the place - was having an immense success. No matter at what hour of the day we passed through that square, there was always the same spellbound circle of half-clad Turks and Arabs squatting silent while "Wagner" tinkled to them on a three-stringed lute and chanted in a high-pitched, dismal whine - like the squeaking of an unfastened door in the wind. At times, for no apparent reason, the never-varying, never-ending measure would be interrupted by a flutter of applause, but his audience remained mostly sunk in a hypnotic apathy. I never see a "Ring" audience now without thinking of that scene outside the Bab-el-Marsa gate, which has led me to ask different people just what sensations serious music produced upon them. The answers have been varied and interesting. One good lady who rarely misses a German opera confessed that sweet sounds acted upon her like opium. Neither scenery nor acting nor plot were of any importance. From the first notes of the overture to the end, she floated in an ecstatic dream, oblivious of time and place. When it was over she came back to herself faint with fatigue. Another professed lover of Wagner said that his greatest pleasure was in following the different "motives" as they recurred in the music. My faith in that gentleman was shaken, however, when I found the other evening that he had mistaken Van Dyck for Jean de Reszke through an entire performance. He may be a dab at recognizing his friends the "motives," but his discoveries don't apparently go as far as tenors!

No one doubts that hundreds of people unaffectedly love German opera, but that as many affect to appreciate it in order to appear intellectual is certain.

Once upon a time the unworthy member of an ultra-serious "Browning" class in this city, doubting the sincerity of her companions, asked permission to read them a poem of the master's which she found beyond her comprehension. When the reading was over the opinion of her friends was unanimous. "Nothing could be simpler! The lines were lucidity itself! Such close reasoning etc." But dismay fell upon them when the naughty lady announced, with a peal of laughter, that she had been reading alternate lines from opposite pages. She no longer disturbs the harmony of that circle!

Bearing this tale in mind, I once asked a musician what proportion of the audience at a "Ring" performance he thought would know if alternate scenes were given from two of Wagner's operas, unless the scenery enlightened them. His estimate was that perhaps fifty per cent might find out the fraud. He put the number of people who could give an intelligent account of those plots at about thirty per hundred.

The popularity of music, he added, is largely due to the fact that it saves people the trouble of thinking. Pleasant sounds soothe the nerves, and, if prolonged long enough in a darkened room will, like the Eastern tom-toms, lull the senses into a mild form of trance. This must be what the gentleman meant who said he wished he could sleep as well in a "Wagner" car as he did at one of his operas!

Being a tailless old fox, I look with ever-increasing suspicion on the too-luxuriant caudal appendages of my neighbors, and think with amusement of the multitudes who during the last ten years have sacrificed themselves upon the altar of grand opera - simple, kindly souls, with little or no taste for classical music, who have sat in the dark (mentally and physically), applauding what they didn't understand, and listening to vague German mythology set to sounds that appear to us outsiders like music sunk into a verbose dotage. I am convinced the greater number would have preferred a jolly performance of Mme.

Angot or the Cloches de Corneville, cut in two by a good ballet.

It is, however, so easy to be mistaken on subjects of this kind that generalizing is dangerous. Many great authorities have liked tuneless music. One of the most telling arguments in its favor was recently advanced by a foreigner. The Chinese ambassador told us last winter in a club at Washington that Wagner's was the only European music that he appreciated and enjoyed. "You see," he added, "music is a much older art with us than in Europe, and has naturally reached a far greater perfection. The German school has made a long step in advance, and I can now foresee a day not far distant when, under its influence, your music will closely resemble our own."

CHAPTER 16

THE POETIC CABARETS OF PARIS

Those who have not lived in France can form little idea of the important place the cafe occupies in the life of an average Frenchman, clubs as we know them or as they exist in England being rare, and when found being, with few exceptions, but gambling-houses in disguise. As a Frenchman rarely asks an acquaintance, or even a friend, to his apartment, the cafe has become the common ground where all meet, for business or pleasure. Not in Paris only, but all over France, in every garrison town, provincial city, or tiny village, the cafe is the chief attraction, the centre of thought, the focus toward which all the rays of masculine existence converge.

For the student, newly arrived from the provinces, to whose modest purse the theatres and other places of amusement are practically closed, the cafe is a supreme resource. His mind is moulded, his ideas and opinions formed, more by what he hears and sees there than by any other influence. A restaurant is of little importance. One may eat anywhere. But the choice of his cafe will often give the bent to a young man's career, and indicate his exact shade of politics and his opinions on literature, music, or art. In Paris, to know a man at all is to know where you can find him at the hour of the aperitif - what Baudelaire called

> L'heure sainte
> De l'absinthe.

When young men form a society among themselves, a cafe is chosen as their meeting-place. Thousands of establishments exist only by such patronage, as, for example, the Cafe de la Regence, Place du Theatre Francais, which is frequented entirely by men who play chess.

Business men transact their affairs as much over their coffee as in their offices. The reading man finds at his cafe the daily and weekly papers; a writer is sure of the undisturbed possession of pen, ink, and paper. Henri Murger, the author, when asked once why he continued to patronize a certain establishment notorious for the inferior quality of its beer, answered, "Yes, the beer is poor, but they keep such good INK!"

The use of a cafe does not imply any great expenditure, a consummation costing but little. With it is acquired the right to use the establishment for an indefinite number of hours, the client being warmed, lighted, and served. From five to seven, and again after dinner, the habitues stroll in, grouping themselves about the small tables, each new-comer joining a congenial circle, ordering his drink, and settling himself for a long sitting. The last editorial, the newest picture, or the fall of a ministry is discussed with a vehemence and an interest unknown to Anglo-Saxon natures. Suddenly, in the excitement of the discussion, some one will rise in his place and begin speaking. If you happen to drop in at that moment, the lady at the desk will welcome you with, "You are just in time! Monsieur So-and-So is speaking; the evening promises to be interesting." She is charmed; her establishment will shine with a reflected light, and new patrons be drawn there, if the debates are brilliant. So universal is this custom that there is hardly an orator to-day at the French bar or in the Senate, who has not broken his first lance in some such obscure tournament, under the smiling glances of the dame du comptoir.

Opposite the Palace of the Luxembourg, in the heart of the old Latin Quarter, stands a quaint building, half hotel, half cafe, where many years ago Joseph II. resided while visiting his sister, Marie Antoinette. It is known now as Foyot's; this name must awaken many happy memories in the hearts of American students, for it was long their favorite meeting-place. In the early seventies a club, formed among the literary and poetic youth of Paris, selected Foyot's as their "home" during the winter months. Their summer vacations were spent in visiting the university towns of France, reciting verses, or acting in original plays at Nancy, Bordeaux, Lyons, or Caen. The enthusiasm these youthful performances created inspired one of their number with the idea of creating in Paris, on a permanent footing, a centre where a limited public could meet the young poets of the day and hear them recite their verses and monologues in an informal way.

The success of the original "Chat Noir," the first cabaret of this kind, was largely owing to the sympathetic and attractive nature of its founder, young Salis, who drew around him, by his sunny disposition, shy personalities who, but for him, would still be "mute, inglorious Miltons." Under his kindly and discriminating rule many a successful literary career has started. Salis's gifted nature combined a delicate taste and critical acumen with a rare business ability. His first venture, an obscure little cafe on the Boulevard Rochechouart, in the outlying quarter beyond the Place Pigalle, quickly became famous, its ever-increasing vogue forcing its happy proprietor to seek more commodious quarters in the rue Victor Masse, where the world-famous "Chat Noir" was installed with much pomp and many joyous ceremonies.

The old word cabaret, corresponding closely to our English "inn," was chosen, and the establishment decorated in imitation of a Louis XIII. hotellerie. Oaken beams supported the low-studded ceilings: The plaster walls disappeared behind tapestries, armor, old faience. Beer and other liquids were served in quaint porcelain or pewter mugs, and the waiters were dressed (merry anachronism) in the costume of members of the Institute (the Immortal Forty), who had so long led poetry in chains. The success of the "Black Cat" in her new quarters was immense, all Paris crowding through her modest doors. Salis had founded Montmartre! - the rugged old hill giving birth to a generation of writers and poets, and nourishing this new school at her granite breasts.

It would be difficult to imagine a form of entertainment more tempting than was offered in this picturesque inn. In addition to the first, the entire second floor of the building had been thrown into one large room, the walls covered with a thousand sketches, caricatures, and crayon drawings by hands since celebrated the world over. A piano, with many chairs and tables, completed the unpretending installation. Here, during a couple of hours each evening, either by the piano or simply standing in their places, the young poets gave utterance to the creations of their imagination, the musicians played their latest inspirations, the raconteur told his newest story. They called each other and the better known among the guests by their names, and joked mutual weaknesses, eliminating from these gatherings every shade of a perfunctory performance.

It is impossible to give an idea of the delicate flavor of such informal evenings - the sensation of being at home that the picturesque surroundings produced, the low murmur of conversation, the clink of glasses, the swing of the waltz movement played by a master hand, interrupted only when some slender form would lean against the piano and pour forth burning words of infinite pathos, - the inspired young face lighted up by the passion and power of the lines. The burst of applause that his talent called forth would hardly have died away before another figure would take the poet's place, a wave of laughter welcoming the new-comer, whose twinkling eyes and demure smile promised a treat of fun and humor. So the evening would wear gayly to its end, the younger element in the audience, full of the future, drinking in long draughts of poetry and art, the elders charmed to live over again the days of their youth and feel in touch once more with the present.

In this world of routine and conventions an innovation as brilliantly successful as this could hardly be inaugurated without raising a whirlwind of jealousy and opposition. The struggle was long and arduous. Directors of theatres and concert halls, furious to see a part of their public tempted away, raised the cry of immorality against the new-comers, and called to their aid every resource of law and chicanery. At the end of the first year Salis found himself with over eight hundred summonses and lawsuits on his hands. After having made every effort, knocked at every door, in his struggle for existence, he finally conceived the happy thought of appealing directly to Grevy, then President of the Republic, and in his audience with the latter succeeded in charming and interesting him, as he had so many others. The influence of the head of the state once brought to bear on the affair, Salis had the joy of seeing opposition crushed and the storm blow itself out.

From this moment, the poets, feeling themselves appreciated and their rights acknowledged and defended, flocked to the "Sacred Mountain," as Montmartre began to be called; other establishments of the same character sprang up in the neighborhood. Most important among these were the "4 z'Arts," Boulevard de Clichy, the "Tambourin," and La Butte.

Trombert, who, together with Fragerolle, Goudezki, and Marcel Lefevre, had just ended an artistic voyage in the south of France, opened the "4 z'Arts," to which the novelty-loving public quickly found its way, crowding to applaud Coquelin cadet, Fragson, and other budding celebrities. It was here that the poets first had the idea of producing a piece in which rival cabarets were reviewed and laughingly criticised. The success was beyond all precedent, in spite of the difficulty of giving a play without a stage, without scenery or accessories of any kind, the interest centring in the talent with which the lines were declaimed by their authors, who next had the pleasant thought of passing in review the different classes of popular songs, Clovis Hugues, at the same time poet and states-man, discoursing on each subject, and introducing the singer; Brittany local songs, Provencal ballads, ant the half Spanish, half French chansons of the Pyrenees were sung or recited by local poets with the charm and abandon of their distinctive races.

The great critics did not disdain to attend these informal gatherings, nor to write columns of serious criticism on the subject in their papers.

At the hour when all Paris takes its aperitif the "4 z'Arts" became the meeting-place of the painters, poets, and writers of the day. Montmartre gradually replaced the old Latin Quarter; it is there to-day that one must seek for the gayety and humor, the pathos and the makeshifts of Bohemia.

The "4 z'Arts," next to the "Chat Noir," has had the greatest influence on the taste of our time, - the pleiad of poets that grouped themselves around it in the beginning, dispersing later to form other centres, which, in their turn, were to influence the minds and moods of thousands.

Another charming form of entertainment inaugurated by this group of men is that of "shadow pictures," conceived originally by Caran d'Ache, and carried by him to a marvellous perfection. A medium-sized frame filled with ground glass is suspended at one end of a room and surrounded by sombre draperies. The room is darkened; against the luminous background of the glass appear small black groups (shadows cast by figures cut out of cardboard). These figures move, advancing and retreating, grouping or separating themselves to the cadence of the poet's verses, for which they form the most original and striking illustrations. Entire poems are given accompanied by these shadow pictures.

One of Caran d'Ache's greatest successes in this line was an Epopee de Napoleon, - the great Emperor appearing on foot and on horseback, the long lines of his army passing before him in the foreground or small in the distance. They stormed heights, cheered on by his presence, or formed hollow squares to repulse the enemy. During their evolutions, the clear voice of the poet rang out from the darkness with thrilling effect.

The nicest art is necessary to cut these little figures to the required perfection. So great was the talent of their inventor that, when he gave burlesques of the topics of the day, or presented the celebrities of the hour to his public, each figure would be recognized with a burst of delighted applause. The great Sarah was represented in poses of infinite humor, surrounded by her menagerie or receiving the homage of the universe. Political leaders, foreign sovereigns, social and operatic stars, were made to pass before a laughing public. None were spared. Paris went mad with delight at this new "art," and for months it was impossible to find a seat vacant in the hall.

At the Boite a Musique, the idea was further developed. By an ingenious arrangement of lights, of which the secret has been carefully kept, landscapes are represented in color; all the gradations of light are given, from the varied twilight hues to purple night, until the moon, rising, lights anew the picture. During all these variations of color little groups continue to come and go, acting out the story of a poem, which the poet delivers from the surrounding obscurity as only an author can render his own lines.

One of the pillars of this attractive centre was Jules Jouy, who made a large place for himself in the hearts of his contemporaries - a true poet, whom neither privations nor the difficult beginnings of an unknown writer could turn from his vocation. His songs are alternately tender, gay, and bitingly sarcastic. Some of his better-known ballads were written for and marvellously interpreted by Yvette Guilbert. The difficult critics, Sarcey and Jules Lemaitre, have sounded his praise again and again.

A cabaret of another kind which enjoyed much celebrity, more on account of the personality of the poet who founded it than from any originality or picturesqueness in its intallation, was the "Mirliton," opened by Aristide Bruant in the little rooms that had sheltered the original "Chat Noir."

To give an account of the "Mirliton" is to tell the story of Bruant, the most popular ballad-writer in France to-day. This original and eccentric poet is as well-known to a Parisian as the boulevards or the Arc de Triomphe. His costume of shabby black velvet, Brittany waist-oat, red shirt, top-boots, and enormous hat is a familiar feature in the caricatures and prints of the day. His little cabaret remains closed during the day, opening its doors toward evening. The personality of the ballad-writer pervades the atmosphere. He walks about the tiny place hailing his acquaintances with some gay epigram, receiving strangers with easy familiarity or chilling disdain, as the humor takes him; then in a moment, with a rapid change of expression, pouring out the ringing lines of one of his ballads - always the story of the poor and humble, for he has identified himself with the outcast and the disinherited. His volumes Dans la Rue and Sur la Route have had an enormous popularity, their contents being known and sung all over France.

In 1892 Bruant was received as a member of the society of Gens de Lettres. It may be of interest to recall a part of the speech made by Francois Coppee on the occasion: "It is with the greatest pleasure that I present to my confreres my good friend, the ballad-writer, Aristide Bruant. I value highly the author of Dans la Rue. When I close his volume of sad and caustic verses it is with the consoling thought that even vice and crime have their conscience: that if there is suffering there is a possible redemption. He has sought his inspiration in the gutter, it is true, but he has seen there a reflection of the stars."

In the Avenue Trudaine, not far from the other cabarets, the "Ane Rouge" was next opened, in a quiet corner of the immense suburb, its shady-little garden, on which the rooms open, making it a favorite meeting-place during the warm months. Of a summer evening no more congenial spot can be found in all Paris. The quaint chambers have been covered with mural paintings or charcoal caricatures of the poets themselves, or of familiar faces among the clients and patrons of the place.

One of the many talents that clustered around this quiet little garden was the brilliant Paul Verlaine, the most Bohemian of all inhabitants of modern Prague, whose death has left a void, difficult to fill. Fame and honors came too late. He died in destitution, if not absolutely of hunger; to-day his admirers are erecting a bronze bust of him in the Garden of the Luxembourg, with money that would have gone far toward making his life happy.

In the old hotel of the Lesdiguieres family, rue de la Tour d'Auvergne, the "Carillon" opened its doors in 1893, and quickly conquered a place in the public favor, the inimitable fun and spirits of Tiercy drawing crowds to the place.

The famous "Treteau de Tabarin," which to-day holds undisputed precedence over all the cabarets of Paris, was among the last to appear. It was founded by the brilliant Fursy and a group of his friends. Here no pains have been spared to form a setting worthy of the poets and their public.

Many years ago, in the days of the good king Louis XIII., a strolling poet-actor, Tabarin, erected his little canvas-covered stage before the statue of Henry IV., on the Pont-Neuf, and drew the court and the town by his fun and pathos. The founders of the latest and most complete of Parisian cabarets have reconstructed, as far as possible, this historic scene. On the wall of the room where the performances are given, is painted a view of old Paris, the Seine and its bridges, the towers of Notre Dame in the distance, and the statue of Louis XIII.'s warlike father in the foreground. In front of this painting stands a staging of rough planks, reproducing the little theatre of Tabarin. Here, every evening, the authors and poets play in their own pieces, recite their verses, and tell their stories. Not long ago a young musician, who has already given an opera to the world, sang an entire one-act operetta of his composition, changing his voice for the different parts, imitating choruses by clever effects on the piano.

Montmartre is now sprinkled with attractive cabarets, the taste of the public for such informal entertainments having grown each year; with reason, for the careless grace of the surroundings, the absence of any useless restraint or obligation as to hour or duration, has a charm for thousands whom a long concert or the inevitable five acts at the Francais could not tempt. It would be difficult to overrate the influence such an atmosphere, breathed in youth, must have on the taste and character. The absence of a sordid spirit, the curse of our material day and generation, the contact with intellects trained to incase their thoughts in serried verse or crisp and lucid prose, cannot but form the hearer's mind into a higher and better mould. It is both a satisfaction and a hope for the future to know that these influences are being felt all over the capital and throughout the length and breadth of France. There are at this moment in Paris alone three or four hundred poets, ballad writers, and raconteurs who recite their works in public.

It must be hard for the untravelled Anglo-Saxon to grasp the idea that a poet can, without loss of prestige, recite his lines in a public cafe before a mixed audience. If such doubting souls could, however, be present at one of these noctes ambrosianae, they would acknowledge that the Latin temperament can throw a grace and child-like abandon around an act that would cause an Englishman or an American to appear supremely ridiculous. One's taste and sense of fitness are never shocked. It seems the most natural thing in the world to be sitting with your glass of beer before you, while some rising poet, whose name ten years later may figure among the "Immortal Forty," tells to you his loves and his ambition, or brings tears into your eyes with a description of some humble hero or martyr.

From the days of Homer poetry has been the instructor

of nations. In the Orient to-day the poet story-teller holds his audience spellbound for hours, teaching the people their history and supplying their minds with food for thought, raising them above the dull level of the brutes by the charm of his verse and the elevation of his ideas. The power of poetry is the same now as three thousand years ago. Modern skeptical Paris, that scoffs at all creeds and chafes impatiently under any rule, will sit to-day docile and complaisant, charmed by the melody of a poet's voice; its passions lulled or quickened, like Alexander's of old, at the will of a modern Timotheus.

CHAPTER 17

ETIQUETTE AT HOME AND ABROAD

Reading that a sentinel had been punished the other day at St. Petersburg for having omitted to present arms, as her Imperial Highness, the Grand Duchess Olga, was leaving the winter palace - in her nurse's arms - I smiled at what appeared to be needless punctilio; then, as is my habit, began turning the subject over, and gradually came to the conclusion that while it could doubtless be well to suppress much of the ceremonial encumbering court life, it might not be amiss if we engrafted a little more etiquette into our intercourse with strangers and the home relations. In our dear free and easy-going country there is a constant tendency to loosen the ties of fireside etiquette until any manners are thought good enough, as any toilet is considered sufficiently attractive for home use. A singular impression has grown up that formal politeness and the saying of gracious and compli-mentary things betray the toady and the hypocrite, both if whom are abhorrent to Americans.

By the force of circumstances most people are civil enough in general society; while many fail to keep to their high standard in the intimacy of home life and in their intercourse with inferiors, which is a pity, as these are the two cases where self-restraint and amenity are most required. Politeness is, after all, but the dictate of a kind heart, and supplies the oil necessary to make the social machinery run smoothly. In home life, which is the association during many hours each day of people of varying dispositions, views, and occupations, friction is inevitable; and there is especial need of lubrication to lessen the wear and tear and eliminate jarring.

Americans are always much shocked to learn that we are not popular on the Continent. Such a discovery comes to either a nation or an individual like a douche of cold water on nice, warm conceit, and brings with it a feeling of discouragement, of being unjustly treated, that is painful, for we are very "touchy" in America, and cry out when a foreigner expresses anything but admiration for our ways, yet we are the last to lend ourselves to foreign customs.

It has been a home thrust for many of us to find that our dear friends the French sympathized warmly with Spain in the recent struggle, and had little but sneers for us. One of the reasons for this partiality is not hard to discover.

The Spanish who travel are mostly members of an aristocracy celebrated for its grave courtesy, which has gone a long way toward making them popular on the Continent, while we have for years been riding rough-shod over the feelings and prejudices of the European peoples, under the pleasing but fallacious illusion that the money we spent so lavishly in foreign lands would atone for all our sins. The large majority of our travelling compatriots forget that an elaborate etiquette exists abroad regulating the intercourse between one class and another, the result of centuries of civilization, and as the Medic and Persian laws for durability. In our ignorance we break many of these social laws and give offence where none was intended.

A single illustration will explain my meaning. A young American girl once went to the mistress of a pension where she was staying and complained that the concierge of the house had been impertinent. When the proprietress asked the concierge what this meant, the latter burst out with her wrongs. "Since Miss B. has been in this house, she has never once bowed to me, or addressed a word to either my husband or myself that was not a question or an order; she walks in and out of my loge to look for letters or take her key as though my room were the street; I won't stand such treatment from any one, much less from a girl. The duchess who lives au quatrieme never passes without a kind word or an inquiry after the children or my health."

Now this American girl had erred through ignorance of the fact that in France servants are treated as humble friends. The man who brings your matutinal coffee says "Good morning" on entering the room, and inquires if "Monsieur has slept well," expecting to be treated with the same politeness he shows to you.

The lady who sits at the caisse of the restaurant you frequent is as sure of her position as her customers are of theirs, and exacts a courteous salutation from every one entering or leaving her presence; logically, for no gentleman would enter a ladies' drawing-room without removing his hat. The fact that a woman is obliged to keep a shop in no way relieves him of this obligation.

People on the Continent know their friends' servants by name, and speak to them on arriving at a house, and thank them for an opened door or offered coat; if a tip is given it is accompanied by a gracious word. So rare is this form of civility in America and England (for Britons err as gravely in this matter as ourselves) that our servants are surprised and inclined to resent politeness, as in the case of an English butler who recently came to his master and said he should be "obliged to leave." On being questioned it came out that one of the guests was in the habit of chatting with him, "and," added the Briton, "I won't stand being took liberties with by no one."

Some years ago I happened to be standing in the vestibule of the Hotel Bristol as the Princess of Wales and her daughters were leaving. Mr. Morlock, the proprietor, was at the foot of the stairs to take leave of those ladies, who shook hands with and thanked him for his attention during their stay, and for the flowers he had sent. Nothing could have been more gracious and freer from condescension than their manner, and it undoubtedly produced the best impression. The waiter who served me at that time was also under their charm, and remarked several times that "there had never been ladies so easy to please or so considerate of the servants."

My neighbor at dinner the other evening confided to me that she was "worn out being fitted." "I had such an unpleasant experience this morning," she added. "The jupiere could not get one of my skirts to hang properly. After a dozen attempts I told her to send for the forewoman, when, to my horror, the girl burst out crying, and said she should lose her place if I did. I was very sorry for her, but what else could I do?" It does not seem as if that lady could be very popular with inferiors, does it?

That it needs a lighter hand and more tact to deal with tradespeople than with equals is certain, and we are sure to be the losers when we fail. The last time I was in the East a friend took me into the bazaars to see a carpet he was anxious to buy. The price asked was out of all proportion to its value, but we were gravely invited by the merchant to be seated and coffee was served, that bargaining (which is the backbone of Oriental trade) might be carried on at leisure. My friend, nervous and impatient, like all our race, turned to me and said, "What's all this tomfoolery? Tell him I'll give so much for his carpet; he can take it or leave it." When this was interpreted to the bearded tradesman, he smiled and came down a few dollars in his price, and ordered more coffee. By this time we were outside his shop, and left without the carpet simply because my friend could not conform to the customs of the country he was visiting. The sale of his carpet was a big affair for the Oriental; he intended to carry it through with all the ceremony the occasion required, and would sooner not make a sale than be hustled out of his stately routine.

It is not only in intercourse with inferiors that tact is required. The treatment of children and young people in a family calls for delicate handling. The habit of taking liberties with young relations is a common form of a relaxed social code and the besetting sin of elderly people, who, having little to interest them in their own lives, imagine that their mission is to reform the ways and manners of their family. Ensconced behind the respect which the young are supposed to pay them, they give free vent to inclination, and carp, cavil, and correct. The victims may have reached maturity or even middle age, but remain always children to these social policemen, to be reproved and instructed in and out of season. "I am doing this for your own good," is an excuse that apparently frees the veterans from the necessity of respecting the prejudices and feelings of their pupils, and lends a gloss of unselfishness to actions which are simply impertinent. Oddly enough, amateur "schoolmarms" who fall into this unpleasant habit are generally oversensitive, and resent as a personal affront any restlessness under criticism on the part of their victims. It is easy, once the habit is acquired, to carry the suavity and consideration of general society into the home circle, yet how often is it done? I should like to see the principle that ordered presentation of arms to the infant princess applied to our intimate relations, and the rights of the young and dependent scrupulously respected.

In the third act of Caste, when old Eccles steals the "coral" from his grandson's neck, he excuses the theft by a grandiloquent soliloquy, and persuades himself that he is protecting "the weak and the humble" (pointing to himself) "against the powerful and the strong" (pointing to the baby). Alas, too many of us take liberties with those whom we do not fear, and excuse our little acts of cowardice with arguments as fallacious as those of drunken old Eccles.

CHAPTER 18

WHAT IS "ART"?

In former years, we inquiring youngsters in foreign studios were much bewildered by the repetition of a certain phrase. Discussion of almost any picture or statue was (after other forms of criticism had been exhausted) pretty sure to conclude with, "It's all very well in its way, but it's not Art." Not only foolish youths but the "masters" themselves constantly advanced this opinion to crush a rival or belittle a friend. To ardent minds seeking for the light and catching at every thread that might serve as a guide out of perplexity, this vague assertion was confusing. According to one master, the eighteenth-century "school" did not exist. What had been produced at that time was pleasing enough to the eye, but "was not Art!" In the opinion of another, Italian music might amuse or cheer the ignorant, but could not be recognized by serious musicians.

As most of us were living far from home and friends for the purpose of acquiring the rudiments of art, this continual sweeping away of our foundations was discouraging. What was the use, we sometimes asked ourselves, of toiling, if our work was to be cast contemptuously aside by the next "school" as a pleasing trifle, not for a moment to be taken seriously?

How was one to find out the truth? Who was to decide when doctors disagreed? Where was the rock on which an earnest student might lay his cornerstone without the misgiving that the next wave in public opinion would sap its base and cast him and his ideals out again at sea?

The eighteenth-century artists and the Italian composers had been sincere and convinced that they were producing works of art. In our own day the idol of one moment becomes the jest of the next. Was there, then, no fixed law?

The short period, for instance, between 1875 and the present time has been long enough for the talent of one painter (Bastien-Lepage) to be discovered, discussed, lauded, acclaimed, then gradually forgotten and decried. During the years when we were studying in Paris, that young painter's works were pronounced by the critics and their following to be the last development of Art. Museums and amateurs vied with each other in acquiring his canvases. Yet, only this spring, while dining with two or three art critics in the French capital, I heard Lepage's name mentioned and his works recalled with the smile that is accorded to those who have hoodwinked the public and passed off spurious material as the real thing.

If any one doubts the fleeting nature of a reputation, let him go to a sale of modern pictures and note the prices brought by the favorites of twenty years ago. The paintings of that arch-priest, Meissonier, no longer command the sums that eager collectors paid for them a score of years back. When a great European critic dares assert, as one has recently, of the master's "1815," that "everything in the picture appears metallic, except the cannon and the men's helmets," the mighty are indeed fallen! It is much the same thing with the old masters. There have been fashions in them as in other forms of art. Fifty years ago Rembrandt's work brought but small prices, and until Henri Rochefort (during his exile) began to write up the English school, Romneys, Lawrences, and Gainsboroughs had little market value.

The result is that most of us are as far away from the solution of that vexed question "What is Art?" at forty as we were when boys. The majority have arranged a compromise with their consciences. We have found out what we like (in itself no mean achievement), and beyond such personal preference, are shy of asserting (as we were fond of doing formerly) that such and such works are "Art," and such others, while pleasing and popular, lack the requisite qualities.

To enquiring minds, sure that an answer to this question exists, but uncertain where to look for it, the fact that one of the thinkers of the century has, in a recent "Evangel," given to the world a definition of "Art," the result of many years' meditation, will be received with joy. "Art," says Tolstoi, "is simply a condition of life. It is any form of expression that a human being employs to communicate an emotion he has experienced to a fellow-mortal."

An author who, in telling his hopes and sorrows, amuses or saddens a reader, has in just so much produced a work of art. A lover who, by the sincerity of his accent, communicates the flame that is consuming him to the object of his adoration; the shopkeeper who inspires a purchaser with his own admiration for an object on sale; the baby that makes its joy known to a parent - artists! artists! Brown, Jones, or Robinson, the moment he has consciously produced on a neighbor's ear or eye the sensation that a sound or a combination of colors has effected on his own organs, is an artist!

Of course much of this has been recognized through all time. The formula in which Tolstoi has presented his meditations to the world is, however, so fresh that it comes like a revelation, with the additional merit of being understood, with little or no mental effort, by either the casual reader, who, with half-attention attracted by a headline, says to himself, "'What is art?' That looks interesting!" and skims lightly down the lines, or the thinker who, after perusing Tolstoi's lucid words, lays down the volume with a sigh, and murmurs in his humiliation, "Why have I been all these years seeking in the clouds for what was lying ready at my hand?"

The wide-reaching definition of the Russian writer has the effect of a vigorous blow from a pickaxe at the foundations of a shaky and too elaborate edifice. The wordy superstructure of aphorisms and paradox falls to the ground, disclosing fair "Truth," so long a captive within the temple erected in her honor. As, however, the newly freed goddess smiles on the ignorant and the pedants alike, the result is that with one accord the aesthetes raise a howl! "And the 'beautiful,'" they say, "the beautiful? Can there be any 'Art' without the 'Beautiful'? What! the little greengrocer at the corner is an artist because, forsooth, he has arranged some lettuce and tomatoes into a tempting pile! Anathema! Art is a secret known only to the initiated few; the vulgar can neither understand nor appreciate it! We are the elect! Our mission is to explain what Art is and point out her beauty to a coarse and heedless world. Only those with a sense of the 'beautiful' should be allowed to enter into her sacred presence."

Here the expounders of "Art" plunge into a sea of words, offering a dozen definitions each more obscure than its predecessor, all of which have served in turn as watchwords of different "schools." Tolstoi's sweeping truth is too far-reaching to please these gentry. Like the priests of past religions, they would have preferred to keep such knowledge as they had to themselves and expound it, little at a time, to the ignorant. The great Russian has kicked away their altar and routed the false gods, whose acolytes will never forgive him.

Those of my readers who have been intimate with painters, actors, or musicians, will recall with amusement how lightly the performances of an associate are condemned by the brotherhood as falling short of the high standard which according to these wiseacres, "Art" exacts, and how sure each speaker is of understanding just where a brother carries his "mote."

Voltaire once avoided giving a definition of the beautiful by saying, "Ask a toad what his ideas of beauty are. He will indicate the particular female toad he happens to admire and praise her goggle-eyes and yellow belly as the perfection of beauty!" A negro from Guiana will make much the same unsatisfactory answer, so the old philosopher recommends us not to be didactic on subjects where judgments are relative, and at the same time without appeal.

Tolstoi denies that an idea as subtle as a definition of Art can be classified by pedants, and proceeds to formulate the following delightful axiom: "A principle upon which no two people can agree does not exist." A truth is proved by its evidence to all. Discussion outside of that is simply beating the air. Each succeeding "school" has sounded its death-knell by asserting that certain combinations alone produced beauty - the weakness of to-day being an inclination to see art only in the obscure and the recondite. As a result we drift each hour further from the truth. Modern intellectuality has formed itself into a scornful aristocracy whose members, esteeming themselves the elite, withdraw from the vulgar public, and live in a world of their own, looking (like the Lady of Shalott) into a mirror at distorted images of nature and declaring that what they see is art!

In literature that which is difficult to understand is much admired by the simple-minded, who also decry pictures that tell their own story! A certain class of minds enjoy being mystified, and in consequence writers, painters, and musicians have appeared who are willing to juggle for their amusement. The simple definition given to us by the Russian writer comes like a breath of wholesome air to those suffocating in an atmosphere of perfumes and artificial heat. Art is our common inheritance, not the property of a favored few. The wide world we love is full of it, and each of us in his humble way is an artist when with a full heart he communicates his delight and his joy to another. Tolstoi has given us back our birthright, so long withheld, and crowned with his aged hands the true artist.

CHAPTER 19

THE GENEALOGICAL CRAZE

There undoubtedly is something in the American temperament that prevents our doing anything in moderation. If we take up an idea, it is immediately run to exaggeration and then abandoned, that the nation may fly at a tangent after some new fad. Does this come from our climate, or (as I am inclined to think) from the curiously unclassified state of society in our country, where so few established standards exist and so few are sure of their own or their neighbors' standing? In consequence, if Mrs. Brown starts anything, Mrs. Jones, for fear of being left behind, immediately "goes her one better" to be in turn "raised" by Mrs. Robinson.

In other lands a reasonable pride of birth has always been one of the bonds holding communities together, and is estimated at its just value. We, after having practically ignored the subject for half a century, suddenly rush to the other extreme, and develop an entire forest of genealogical trees at a growth.

Chagrined, probably, at the small amount of consideration that their superior birth commanded, a number of aristocratically minded matrons united a few years ago as "Daughters of the Revolution," restricting membership to women descended from officers of Washington's army. There may have been a reason for the formation of this society. I say "may" because it does not seem quite clear what its aim was. The originators doubtless imagined they were founding an exclusive circle, but the numbers who clamored for admittance quickly dispelled this illusion. So a small group of the elect withdrew in disgust and banded together under the cognomen of "Colonial Dames."

The only result of these two movements was to awaken envy, hatred, and malice in the hearts of those excluded from the mysterious rites, which to outsiders seemed to consist in blackballing as many aspirants as possible. Some victims of this bad treatment, thirsting for revenge, struck on the happy thought of inaugurating an "Aztec" society. As that title conveyed absolutely no idea to any one, its members were forced to explain that only descendants of officers who fought in the Mexican War were eligible. What the elect did when they got into the circle was not specified.

The "Social Order of Foreign Wars" was the next creation, its authors evidently considering the Mexican campaign as a domestic article, a sort of family squabble. Then the "Children of 1812" attracted attention, both groups having immediate success. Indeed, the vogue of these enterprises has been in inverse ratio to their usefulness or raison d'etre, people apparently being ready to join anything rather than get left out in the cold.

Jealous probably of seeing women enjoying all the fun, their husbands and brothers next banded together as "Sons of the Revolution." The wives retaliated by instituting the "Granddaughters of the Revolution" and

"The Mayflower Order," the "price of admission" to the latter being descent from some one who crossed in that celebrated ship - whether as one of the crew or as passenger is not clear.

It was not, however, in the American temperament to rest content with modest beginnings, the national motto being, "The best is good enough for me." So wind was quickly taken out of the Mayflower's sails by "The Royal Order of the Crown," to which none need apply who were not prepared to prove descent from one or more royal ancestors. It was not stated in the prospectus whether Irish sovereigns and Fiji Island kings counted, but I have been told that bar sinisters form a class apart, and are deprived of the right to vote or hold office.

Descent from any old king was, however, not sufficient for the high-toned people of our republic. When you come to think of it, such a circle might be "mixed." One really must draw the line somewhere (as the Boston parvenu replied when asked why he had not invited his brother to a ball). So the founders of the "Circle of Holland Dames of the New Netherlands" drew the line at descent from a sovereign of the Low Countries. It does not seem as if this could be a large society, although those old Dutch pashas had an unconscionable number of children.

The promoters of this enterprise seem nevertheless to have been fairly successful, for they gave a fete recently and crowned a queen. To be acclaimed their sovereign by a group of people all of royal birth is indeed an honor. Rumors of this ceremony have come to us outsiders. It is said that they employed only lineal descendants of Vatel to prepare their banquet, and I am assured that an offspring of Gambrinus acted as butler.

But it is wrong to joke on this subject. The state of affairs is becoming too serious. When sane human beings form a "Baronial Order of Runnymede," and announce in their prospectus that only descendants through the male line from one (or more) of the forty noblemen who forced King John to sign the Magna Charta are what our Washington Mrs. Malaprop would call "legible," the action attests a diseased condition of the community. Any one taking the trouble to remember that eight of the original barons died childless, and that the Wars of the Roses swept away nine tenths of what families the others may have had, that only one man in England (Lord de Ros) can at the present day PROVE male descent further back than the eleventh century, must appreciate the absurdity of our compatriots' pretensions. Burke's Peerage is acknowledged to be the most "faked" volume in the English language, but the descents it attributes are like mathematical demonstrations compared to the "trees" that members of these new American orders climb.

When my class was graduated from Mr. McMullen's school, we little boys had the brilliant idea of uniting in a society, but were greatly put about for an effective name, hitting finally upon that of Ancient Seniors' Society. For a group of infants, this must be acknowledged to have been a luminous inspiration. We had no valid reason for forming that society, not being particularly fond of each other. Living in several cities, we rarely met after leaving school and had little to say to each other when we did. But it sounded so fine to be an "Ancient Senior," and we hoped in our next school to impress new companions with that title and make them feel proper respect for us in consequence. Pride, however, sustained a fall when it was pointed out that the initials formed the ominous word "Ass."

I have a shrewd suspicion that the motives which prompted our youthful actions are not very different from those now inciting children of a larger growth to band together, blackball their friends, crown queens, and perform other senseless mummeries, such as having the weathercock of a departed meeting-house brought in during a banquet, and dressing restaurant waiters in knickerbockers for "one night only."

This malarial condition of our social atmosphere accounts for the quantity of genealogical quacks that have taken to sending typewritten letters, stating that the interest they take in your private affairs compels them to offer proof of your descent from any crowned head to whom you may have taken a fancy. One correspondent assured me only this month that he had papers in his possession showing beyond a doubt that I might claim a certain King McDougal of Scotland for an ancestor. I have misgivings, however, as to the quality of the royal blood in my veins, for the same correspondent was equally confident six months ago that my people came in direct line from Charlemagne. As I have no desire to "corner" the market in kings, these letters have remained unanswered.

Considering the mania to trace descent from illustrious men, it astonishes me that a Mystic Band, consisting of lineal descendants from the Seven Sages of Greece, has not before now burst upon an astonished world. It has been suggested that if some one wanted to organize a truly restricted circle, "The Grandchildren of our Tripoli War" would be an excellent title. So few Americans took part in that conflict - and still fewer know anything about it - that the satisfaction of joining the society would be immense to exclusively-minded people.

There is only one explanation that seems in any way to account for this vast tomfoolery. A little sentence, printed at the bottom of a prospectus recently sent to me, lets the ambitious cat out of the genealogical bag. It states that "social position is assured to people joining our order." Thanks to the idiotic habit some newspapers have inaugurated of advertising, gratis, a number of self-elected society "leaders," many feeble-minded people, with more ambition than cash, and a larger supply of family papers than brains, have been bitten with a social madness, and enter these traps, thinking they are the road to position and honors. The number of fools is larger than one would have believed possible, if the success of so many "orders," "circles," "commanderies," and "regencies" were not there to testify to the unending folly of the would-be "smart."

This last decade of the century has brought to light many strange fads and senseless manias. This "descent" craze, however, surpasses them all in inanity. The keepers of insane asylums will tell you that one of the hopeless forms of madness is la folie des grandeurs. A breath of this delirium seems to be blowing over our country. Crowns and sceptres haunt the dreams of simple republican men and women, troubling their slumbers and leading them a will-o'-the-wisp dance back across the centuries.

CHAPTER 20

AS THE TWIG IS BENT

I knew, in my youth, a French village far up among the Cevennes Mountains, where the one cultivated man of the place, saddened by the unlovely lives of the peasants around him and by the bare walls of the village school, organized evening classes for the boys. During these informal hours, he talked to them of literature and art and showed them his prints and paintings. When the youths' interest was aroused he lent them books, that they might read about the statues and buildings that had attracted their attention. At first it appeared a hopeless task to arouse any interest among these peasants in subjects not bearing on their abject lives. To talk with boys of the ideal, when their poor bodies were in need of food and raiment, seemed superfluous; but in time the charm worked, as it always will. The beautiful appealed to their simple natures, elevating and refining them, and opening before their eager eyes perspectives of undreamed-of interest. The self-imposed task became a delight as his pupils' minds responded to his efforts. Although death soon ended his useful life, the seed planted grew and bore fruit in many humble homes.

At this moment I know men in several walks of life who revere with touching devotion the memory of the one human being who had brought to them, at the moment when they were most impressionable, the gracious message that existence was not merely a struggle for bread. The boys he had gathered around him realize now that the encouragement and incentive received from those evening glimpses of noble works existing in the world was the mainspring of their subsequent development and a source of infinite pleasure through all succeeding years.

This reference to an individual effort toward cultivating the poor has been made because other delicate spirits are attempting some such task in our city, where quite as much as in the French village schoolchildren stand in need of some message of beauty in addition to the instruction they receive, - some window opened for them, as it were, upon the fields of art, that their eyes when raised from study or play may rest on objects more inspiring than blank walls and the graceless surroundings of street or schoolroom.

We are far too quick in assuming that love of the beautiful is confined to the highly educated; that the poor have no desire to surround themselves with graceful forms and harmonious colors. We wonder at and deplore their crude standards, bewailing the general lack of taste and the gradual reducing of everything to a commonplace money basis. We smile at the efforts toward adornment attempted by the poor, taking it too readily for granted that on this point they are beyond redemption. This error is the less excusable as so little has been done by way of experiment before forming an opinion, - whole classes being put down as inferior beings, incapable of appreciation, before they have been allowed even a glimpse of the works of art that form the daily mental food of their judges.

The portly charlady who rules despotically in my chambers is an example. It has been a curious study to watch her growing interest in the objects that have here for the first time come under her notice; the delight she has come to take in dusting and arranging my belongings, and her enthusiasm at any new acquisition. Knowing how bare her own home was, I felt at first only astonishment at her vivid interest in what seemed beyond her comprehension, but now realize that in some blind way she appreciates the rare and the delicate quite as much as my more cultivated visitors. At the end of one laborious morning, when everything was arranged to her satisfaction, she turned to me her poor, plain face, lighted up with an expression of delight, and exclaimed, "Oh, sir, I do love to work in these rooms! I'm never so happy as when I'm arranging them elegant things!" And, although my pleasure in her pleasure was modified by the discovery that she had taken an eighteenth-century comb to disentangle the fringes of a rug, and broken several of its teeth in her ardor, that she invariably placed a certain Whister etching upside down, and then stood in rapt admiration before it, still, in watching her enthusiasm, I felt a thrill of satisfaction at seeing how her untaught taste responded to a contact with good things.

Here in America, and especially in our city, which we have been at such pains to make as hideous as possible, the schoolrooms, where hundreds of thousands of children pass many hours daily, are one degree more graceless than the town itself; the most artistically inclined child can hardly receive any but unfortunate impressions. The other day a friend took me severely to task for rating our American women on their love of the big shops, and gave me, I confess, an entirely new idea on the subject. "Can't you see," she said, "that the shops here are what the museums abroad are to the poor? It is in them only that certain people may catch glimpses of the dainty and exquisite manufactures of other countries. The little education their eyes receive is obtained during visits to these emporiums."

If this proves so, and it seems probable, it only proves how the humble long for something more graceful than their meagre homes afford.

In the hope of training the younger generations to better standards and less vulgar ideals, a group of ladies are making an attempt to surround our schoolchildren during their impressionable youth with reproductions of historic masterpieces, and have already decorated many schoolrooms in this way. For a modest sum it is possible to tint the bare walls an attractive color - a delight in itself - and adorn them with plaster casts of statues and solar prints of pictures and buildings. The transformation that fifty or sixty dollars judiciously expended in this way produces in a schoolroom is beyond belief, and, as the advertisements say, "must be seen to be appreciated," giving an air of cheerfulness and refinement to the dreariest apartment.

It is hard to make people understand the enthusiasm these decorations have excited in both teachers and pupils. The directress of one of our large schools was telling me of the help and pleasure the prints and casts had been to her; she had given them as subjects for the class compositions, and used them in a hundred different ways as object-lessons. As the children are graduated from room to room, a great variety of high-class subjects can be brought to their notice by varying the decorations.

It is by the eye principally that taste is educated. "We speak with admiration of the eighth sense common among Parisians, and envy them their magic power of combining simple materials into an artistic whole. The reason is that for generations the eyes of those people have been unconsciously educated by the harmonious lines of well-proportioned buildings, finely finished detail of stately colonnade, and shady perspective of quay and boulevard. After years of this subtle training the eye instinctively revolts from the vulgar and the crude. There is little in the poorer quarters of our city to rejoice or refine the senses; squalor and all-pervading ugliness are not least among the curses that poverty entails.

If you have a subject of interest in your mind, it often happens that every book you open, every person you speak with, refers to that topic. I never remember having seen an explanation offered of this phenomenon.

The other morning, while this article was lying half finished on my desk, I opened the last number of a Paris paper and began reading an account of the drama, Les Mauvais Bergers (treating of that perilous subject, the "strikes"), which Sarah Bernhardt had just had the courage to produce before the Paris public. In the third act, when the owner of the factory receives the disaffected hands, and listens to their complaints, the leader of the strike (an intelligent young workman), besides shorter hours and increased pay, demands that recreation rooms be built where the toilers, their wives, and their children may pass unoccupied hours in the enjoyment of attractive surroundings, and cries in conclusion: "We, the poor, need some poetry and some art in our lives, man does not live by bread alone. He has a right, like the rich, to things of beauty!"

In commending the use of decoration as a means of bringing pleasure into dull, cramped lives, one is too often met by the curious argument that taste is innate. "Either people have it or they haven't," like a long nose or a short one, and it is useless to waste good money in trying to improve either. "It would be much more to the point to spend your money in giving the poor children a good roast-beef dinner at Christmas than in placing the bust of Clytie before them." That argument has crushed more attempts to elevate the poor than any other ever advanced. If it were listened to, there would never be any progress made, because there are always thousands of people who are hungry.

When we reflect how painfully ill-arranged rooms or ugly colors affect our senses, and remember that less fortunate neighbors suffer as much as we do from hideous environments, it seems like keeping sunlight from a plant, or fresh air out of a sick-room, to refuse glimpses of the beautiful to the poor when it is in our power to give them this satisfaction with a slight effort. Nothing can be more encouraging to those who occasionally despair of human nature than the good results already obtained by this small attempt in the schools.

We fall into the error of imagining that because the Apollo Belvedere and the Square of St. Mark's have become stale to us by reproduction they are necessarily so to others. The great and the wealthy of the world form no idea of the longing the poor feel for a little variety in their lives. They do not know what they want. They have no standards to guide them, but the desire is there. Let us offer ourselves the satisfaction, as we start off for pleasure trips abroad or to the mountains, of knowing that at home the routine of study is lightened for thousands of children by the counterfeit presentment of the scenes we are enjoying; that, as we float up the Golden Horn or sit in the moonlight by the Parthenon, far away at home some child is dreaming of those fair scenes as she raises her eyes from her task, and is unconsciously imbibing a love of the beautiful, which will add a charm to her humble life, and make the present labors lighter. If the child never lives to see the originals, she will be happier for knowing that somewhere in the world domed mosques mirror themselves in still waters, and marble gods, the handiwork of long-dead nations, stand in the golden sunlight and silently preach the gospel of the beautiful.

CHAPTER 21

SEVEN SMALL DUCHESSES

Since those "precious" days when the habitues of the Hotel Rambouillet first raised social intercourse to the level of a fine art, the morals and manners, the amusements and intrigues of great French ladies have interested the world and influenced the ways of civilized nations. Thanks to Memoirs and Maxims, we are able to reconstruct the life of a seventeenth or eighteenth century noblewoman as completely as German archeologists have rebuilt the temple of the Wingless Victory on the Acropolis from surrounding debris.

Interest in French society has, however, diminished during this century, ceasing almost entirely with the Second Empire, when foreign women gave the tone to a parvenu court from which the older aristocracy held aloof in disgust behind the closed gates of their "hotels" and historic chateaux.

With the exception of Balzac, few writers have drawn authentic pictures of nineteenth-century noblewomen in France; and his vivid portrayals are more the creations of genius than correct descriptions of a caste.

During the last fifty years French aristocrats have

ceased to be factors even in matters social, the sceptre they once held having passed into alien hands, the daughters of Albion to a great extent replacing their French rivals in influencing the ways of the "world," - a change, be it remarked in passing, that has not improved the tone of society or contributed to the spread of good manners.

People like the French nobles, engaged in sulking and attempting to overthrow or boycott each succeeding regime, must naturally lose their influence. They have held aloof so long - fearing to compromise themselves by any advances to the powers that be, and restrained by countless traditions from taking an active part in either the social or political strife - that little by little they have been passed by and ignored; which is a pity, for amid the ruin of many hopes and ambitions they have remained true to their caste and handed down from generation to generation the secret of that gracious urbanity and tact which distinguished the Gallic noblewoman in the last century from the rest of her kind and made her so deft in the difficult art of pleasing - and being pleased.

Within the last few years there have, however, been signs of a change. Young members of historic houses show an amusing inclination to escape from their austere surroundings and resume the place their grandparents abdicated. If it is impossible to rule as formerly, they at any rate intend to get some fun out of existence.

This joyous movement to the front is being made by the young matrons enlisted under the "Seven little duchesses'" banner. Oddly enough, a baker's half-dozen of ducal coronets are worn at this moment, in

France, by small and sprightly women, who have shaken the dust of centuries from those ornaments and sport them with a decidedly modern air!

It is the members of this clique who, in Paris during the spring, at their chateaux in the summer and autumn, and on the Riviera after Christmas, lead the amusements and strike the key for the modern French world.

No one of these light-hearted ladies takes any particular precedence over the others. All are young, and some are wonderfully nice to look at. The Duchesse d'Uzes is, perhaps, the handsomest, good looks being an inheritance from her mother, the beautiful and wayward Duchesse de Chaulme.

There is a vivid grace about the daughter, an intense vitality that suggests some beautiful being of the forest. As she moves and speaks one almost expects to hear the quick breath coming and going through her quivering nostrils, and see foam on her full lips. Her mother's tragic death has thrown a glamor of romance around the daughter's life that heightens the witchery of her beauty.

Next in good looks comes an American, the Duchesse de la Rochefoucauld, although marriage (which, as de Maupassant remarked, is rarely becoming) has not been propitious to that gentle lady. By rights she should have been mentioned first, as her husband outranks, not only all the men of his age, but also his cousin, the old Duc de la Rochefoucauld-Doudeauville, to whom, however, a sort of brevet rank is accorded on account of his years, his wealth, and the high rank of his two wives. It might almost be asserted that our fair compatriot wears the oldest coronet in France. She certainly is mistress of three of the finest chateaux in that country, among which is Miromail, where the family live, and Liancourt, a superb Renaissance structure, a delight to the artist's soul.

The young Duchesse de Brissac runs her two comrades close as regards looks. Brissac is the son of Mme. de Tredern, whom Newporters will remember two years ago, when she enjoyed some weeks of our summer season. Their chateau was built by the Brissac of Henri IV.'s time and is one of the few that escaped uninjured through the Revolution, its vast stone corridors and massive oak ceilings, its moat and battlements, standing to-day unimpaired amid a group of chateaux including Chaumont, Rochecotte, Azay-le-Rideau, Usse, Chenonceau, within "dining" distance of each other, that form a centre of gayety next in importance to Paris and Cannes. In the autumn these spacious castles are filled with joyous bands and their ample stables with horses. A couple of years ago, when the king of Portugal and his suite were entertained at Chaumont for a week of stag-hunting, over three hundred people, servants, and guests, slept under its roof, and two hundred horses were housed in its stables.

The Duc de Luynes and his wife, who was Mlle. de Crussol (daughter of the brilliant Duchesse d'Uzes of Boulanger fame), live at Dampierre, another interesting pile filled with rare pictures, bric-a-brac, and statuary, first among which is Jean Goujon's life-sized statue (in silver) of Louis XIII., presented by that monarch to his favorite, the founder of the house. This gem of the Renaissance stands in an octagonal chamber hung in dark velvet, unique among statues. It has been shown but once in public, at the Loan Exhibition in 1872, when the patriotic nobility lent their treasures to collect a fund for the Alsace-Lorraine exiles.

The Duchesse de Noailles, nee Mlle. de Luynes, is another of this coterie and one of the few French noblewomen who has travelled. Many Americans will remember the visit she made here with her mother some years ago, and the effect her girlish grace produced at that time. The de Noailles' chateau of Maintenon is an inheritance from Louis XIV.'s prudish favorite, who founded and enriched the de Noailles family. The Duc and Duchesse d'Uzes live near by at Bonnelle with the old Duc de Doudeauville, her grandfather, who is also the grandfather of Mme. de Noailles, these two ladies being descended each from a wife of the old duke, the former from the Princesse de Polignac and the latter from the Princesse de Ligne.

The Duchesse de Bisaccia, nee Princesse Radziwill, and the Duchesse d'Harcourt, who complete the circle of seven, also live in this vicinity, where another group of historic residences, including Eclimont and Rambouillet, the summer home of the president, rivals in gayety and hospitality the chateaux of the Loire.

No coterie in England or in this country corresponds at all to this French community. Much as they love to amuse themselves, the idea of meeting any but their own set has never passed through their well-dressed heads. They differ from their parents in that they have broken away from many antiquated habits. Their houses are no longer lay hermitages, and their opera boxes are regularly filled, but no foreigner is ever received, no ambitious parvenu accepted among them.

Ostracism here means not a ten years' exile, but lifelong banishment.

The contrast is strong between this rigor and the enthusiasm with which wealthy new-comers are welcomed into London society or by our own upper crust, so full of unpalatable pieces of dough. This exclusiveness of the titled French reminds me - incongruously enough - of a certain arrangement of graves in a Lenox cemetery, where the members of an old New England family lie buried in a circle with their feet toward its centre. When I asked, many years ago, the reason for this arrangement, a wit of that day - a daughter, by the bye, of Mrs. Stowe - replied, "So that when they rise at the Last Day only members of their own family may face them!"

One is struck by another peculiarity of these French men and women - their astonishing proficiency in les arts d'agrement. Every Frenchwoman of any pretensions to fashion backs her beauty and grace with some art in which she is sure to be proficient. The dowager Duchesse d'Uzes is a sculptor of mark, and when during the autumn Mme. de Tredern gives opera at Brissac, she finds little difficulty in recruiting her troupe from among the youths and maidens under her roof whose musical education has been thorough enough to enable them to sing difficult music in public.

Love of the fine arts is felt in their conversation, in the arrangement and decoration of their homes, and in the interest that an exhibition of pictures or old furniture will excite. Few of these people but are habitues of the Hotel Drouot and conversant with the value and authenticity of the works of art daily sold there. Such elements combine to form an atmosphere that does not exist in any other country, and lends an interest to society in France which it is far from possessing elsewhere.

There is but one way that an outsider can enter this Gallic paradise. By marrying into it! Two of the seven ladies in question lack the quarterings of the rest. Miss Mitchell was only a charming American girl, and the mother of the Princesse Radziwill was Mlle. Blanc of Monte Carlo. However, as in most religions there are ceremonies that purify, so in this case the sacrament of marriage is supposed to have reconstructed these wives and made them genealogically whole.

There is something incongruous to most people in the idea of a young girl hardly out of the schoolroom bearing a ponderous title. The pomp and circumstance that surround historic names connect them (through our reading) with stately matrons playing the "heavy female" roles in life's drama, much as Lady Macbeth's name evokes the idea of a raw-boned mother-in-law sort of person, the reverse of attractive, and quite the last woman in the world to egg her husband on to a crime - unless it were wife murder!

Names like de Chevreuse, or de la Rochefoucauld, seem appropriate only to the warlike amazons of the Fronde, or corpulent kill-joys in powder and court trains of the Mme. Etiquette school; it comes as a shock, on being presented to a group of girlish figures in the latest cut of golfing skirts, who are chattering odds on the Grand Prix in faultless English, to realize that these light-hearted gamines are the present owners of sonorous titles. One shudders to think what would have been the effect on poor Marie Antoinette's priggish mentor could she have foreseen her granddaughter, clad in knickerbockers, running a petroleum tricycle in the streets of Paris, or pedalling "tandem" across country behind some young cavalry officer of her connection.

Let no simple-minded American imagine, however, that these up-to-date women are waiting to welcome him and his family to their intimacy. The world outside of France does not exist for a properly brought up French aristocrat. Few have travelled; from their point of view, any man with money, born outside of France, is a "Rasta," unless he come with diplomatic rank, in which case his position at home is carefully ferreted out before he is entertained. Wealthy foreigners may live for years in Paris, without meeting a single member of this coterie, who will, however, join any new club that promises to be amusing; but as soon as the "Rastas" get a footing, "the seven" and their following withdraw. Puteaux had its day, then the "Polo Club" in the Bois became their rendezvous. But as every wealthy American and "smart" Englishwoman passing the spring in Paris rushed for that too open circle, like tacks toward a magnet, it was finally cut by the "Duchesses," who, together with such attractive aides-de-camp as the Princesse de Poix, Mmes. de Murat, de Morny, and de Broglie, inaugurated last spring "The Ladies' Club of the Acacias," on a tiny island belonging to the "Tir aux Pigeons," which, for the moment, is the fad of its founders.

It must be a surprise to those who do not know French family pride to learn that exclusive as these women are there are cliques in France to-day whose members consider the ladies we have been speaking of as lacking in reserve. Men like Guy de Durfort, Duc de Lorges, or the Duc de Massa, and their womenkind, hold themselves aloof on an infinitely higher plane, associating with very few and scorning the vulgar herd of "smart" people!

It would seem as if such a vigorous weeding out of the unworthy would result in a rather restricted comradeship. Who the "elect" are must become each year more difficult to discern.

Their point of view in this case cannot differ materially from that of the old Methodist lady, who, while she was quite sure no one outside of her own sect could possibly be saved, had grave fears concerning the future of most of the congregation. She felt hopeful only of the clergyman and herself, adding: "There are days when I have me doubts about the minister!"

CHAPTER 22

GROWING OLD UNGRACEFULLY

There comes, we are told, a crucial moment, "a tide" in all lives, that taken at the flood, leads on to fortune. An assertion, by the bye, which is open to doubt. What does come to every one is an hour fraught with warning, which, if unheeded, leads on to folly. This fateful date coincides for most of us with the discovery that we are turning gray, or that the "crow's feet" or our temples are becoming visible realities. The unpleasant question then presents itself: Are we to slip meekly into middle age, or are arms be taken up against our insidious enemy, and the rest of life become a losing battle, fought inch by inch?

In other days it was the men who struggled the hardest against their fate. Up to this century, the male had always been the ornamental member of a family. Caesar, we read, coveted a laurel crown principally because it would help to conceal his baldness. The wigs of the Grand Monarque are historical. It is characteristic of the time that the latter's attempts at rejuvenation should have been taken as a matter of course, while a few years later poor Madame de Pompadour's artifices to retain her fleeting youth were laughed at and decried.

To-day the situation is reversed. The battle, given up by the men - who now accept their fate with equanimity - is being waged by their better halves with a vigor heretofore unknown. So general has this mania become that if asked what one weakness was most characteristic of modern women, what peculiarity marked them as different from their sisters in other centuries, I should unhesitatingly answer, "The desire to look younger than their years."

That people should long to be handsomer or taller or better proportioned than a cruel Providence has made them, is natural enough; but that so much time and trouble should be spent simply in trying to look "young," does seem unreasonable, especially when it is evident to everybody that such efforts must, in the nature of things, be failures. The men or women who do not look their age are rare. In each generation there are exceptions, people who, from one cause or another - generally an excellent constitution - succeed in producing the illusion of youth for a few years after youth itself has flown.

A curious fatality that has the air of a nemesis pursues those who succeed in giving this false appearance. When pointing them out to strangers, their admirers (in order to make the contrast more effective) add a decade or so to the real age. Only last month I was sitting at dinner opposite a famous French beauty, who at fifty succeeds in looking barely thirty. During the meal both my neighbors directed attention to her appearance, and in each case said: "Isn't she a wonder! You know she's over sixty!" So all that poor lady gained by looking youthful was ten years added to her age!

The desire to remain attractive as long as possible is not only a reasonable but a commendable ambition. Unfortunately the stupid means most of our matrons adopt to accomplish this end produce exactly the opposite result.

One sign of deficient taste in our day is this failure to perceive that every age has a charm of its own which can be enhanced by appropriate surroundings, but is lost when placed in an incongruous setting. It saddens a lover of the beautiful to see matrons going so far astray in their desire to please as to pose for young women when they no longer can look the part.

Holmes, in My Maiden Aunt, asks plaintively: -

Why will she train that wintry curl in such a springlike way?

That this folly is in the air to-day, few will dispute. It seems to be perpetrated unconsciously by the greater number, with no particular object in view, simply because other people do it. An unanswerable argument when used by one of the fair sex!

Few matrons stop to think for themselves, or they would realize that by appearing in the same attire as their daughters they challenge a comparison which can only be to their disadvantage, and should be if possible avoided. Is there any disillusion more painful than, on approaching what appeared from a distance to be a young girl, to find one's self face to face with sixty years of wrinkles? That is a modern version of the saying, "an old head on young shoulders," with a vengeance! If mistaken sexagenarians could divine the effect that tired eyes smiling from under false hair, aged throats clasped with collars of pearls, and rheumatic old ribs braced into a semblance of girlish grace, produce on the men for whose benefit such adornments have been arranged, reform would quickly follow. There is something absolutely uncanny in the illusion. The more successful it is, the more weird the effect.

No one wants to see Polonius in the finery of Mercutio. What a sense of fitness demands is, on the contrary, a "make up" in keeping with the role, which does not mean that a woman is to become a frump, but only that she is to make herself attractive in another way.

During the Ancien Regime in France, matters of taste were considered all-important; an entire court would consult on the shade of a brocade, and hail a new coiffure as an event. The great ladies who had left their youth behind never then committed the blunder, so common among our middle-aged ladies, of aping the maidens of the day. They were far too clever for that, and appreciated the advantages to be gained from sombre stuffs and flattering laces. Let those who doubt study Nattier's exquisite portrait of Maria Leczinska. Nothing in the pose or toilet suggests a desire on the painter's part to rejuvenate his sitter. If anything, the queen's age is emphasized as something honorable. The gray hair is simply arranged and partly veiled with black lace, which sets off her delicate, faded face to perfection, but without flattery or fraud.

We find the same view taken of age by the masters of the Renaissance, who appreciated its charm and loved to reproduce its grace.

Queen Elizabeth stands out in history as a woman who

struggled ungracefully against growing old. Her wigs and hoops and farthingales served only to make her ridiculous, and the fact that she wished to be painted without shadows in order to appear "young," is recorded as an aberration of a great mind.

Are there no painters to-day who will whisper to our wives and mothers the secret of looking really lovely, and persuade them to abandon their foolish efforts at rejuvenation?

Let us see some real old ladies once more, as they look at us from miniature and portrait. Few of us, I imagine, but cherish the memory of some such being in the old home, a soft-voiced grandmother, with silvery hair brushed under a discreet and flattering cap, with soft, dark raiment and tulle-wrapped throat. There are still, it is to be hoped, many such lovable women in our land, but at times I look about me in dismay, and wonder who is to take their places when they are gone. Are there to be no more "old ladies"? Will the next generation have to look back when the word "grandmother" is mentioned, to a stylish vision in Parisian apparel, decollete and decked in jewels, or arrayed in cocky little bonnets, perched on tousled curls, knowing jackets, and golfing skirts?

The present horror of anything elderly comes, probably, from the fact that the preceding generation went to the other extreme, young women retiring at forty into becapped old age. Knowing how easily our excitable race runs to exaggeration, one trembles to think what surprises the future may hold, or what will be the next decree of Dame Fashion. Having eliminated the "old lady" from off the face of the earth, how fast shall we continue down the fatal slope toward the ridiculous? Shall we be compelled by a current stronger than our wills to array ourselves each year (the bare thought makes one shudder) in more and more youthful apparel, until corpulent senators take to running about in "sailor suits," and octogenarian business men go "down town" in "pinafores," while belles of sixty or seventy summers appear in Kate Greenaway costumes, and dine out in short-sleeved bibs, which will allow coy glimpses of their cunning old ankles to appear over their socks?

CHAPTER 23

AROUND A SPRING

The greatest piece of good luck that can befall a Continental village is the discovery, within its limits, of a spring supplying some kind of malodorous water. From that moment the entire community, abandoning all other plans, give themselves over to hatching their golden egg, experience having taught them that no other source of prosperity can compare with a source thermale. If the water of the newfound spring, besides having an unpleasant smell, is also hot, then Providence has indeed blessed the township.

The first step is to have the fluid analyzed by a celebrity, and its medicinal qualities duly set forth in a certificate. The second is to get official recognition from the government and the authorization to erect a bath house. Once these preliminaries accomplished, the way lies plain before the fortunate village; every citizen, from the mayor down to the humblest laborer, devotes himself to solving the all-important problem how to attract strangers to the place and keep and amuse them when they have been secured.

Multicolored pamphlets detailing the local attractions are mailed to the four corners of the earth, and brilliant chromos of the village, with groups of peasants in the foreground, wearing picturesque costumes, are posted in every available railway station and booking-office, regardless of the fact that no costumes have been known in the neighborhood for half a century, except those provided by the hotel proprietors for their housemaids. A national dress, however, has a fine effect in the advertisement, and gives a local color to the scene. What, for instance, would Athens be without that superb individual in national get-up whom one is sure to see before the hotel on alighting from the omnibus? I am convinced that he has given as much pleasure as the Acropolis to most travellers; the knowledge that the hotel proprietors share the expenses of his keep and toilet cannot dispel the charm of those scarlet embroideries and glittering arms.

After preparing their trap, the wily inhabitants of a new watering-place have only to sit down and await events. The first people to appear on the scene are, naturally, the English, some hidden natural law compelling that race to wander forever in inexpensive by-ways and serve as pioneers for other nations. No matter how new or inaccessible the spring, you are sure to find a small colony of Britons installed in the half-finished hotels, reading week-old editions of the Times, and grumbling over the increase in prices since the year before.

As soon as the first stray Britons have developed into an "English colony," the municipality consider themselves authorized to construct a casino and open avenues, which are soon bordered by young trees and younger villas. In the wake of the English come invalids of other nationalities. If a wandering "crowned head" can be secured for a season, a great step is gained, as that will attract the real paying public and the Americans, who as a general thing are the last to appear on the scene.

At this stage of its evolution, the "city fathers" build a theatre in connection with their casino, and (persuading the government to wink at their evasion of the gambling laws) add games of chance to the other temptations of the place.

There is no better example of the way a spring can be developed by clever handling, and satisfactory results obtained from advertising and judicious expenditure, than Aix-les-Bains, which twenty years ago was but a tiny mountain village, and to-day ranks among the wealthiest and most brilliant eaux in Europe. In this case, it is true, they had tradition to fall back on, for Aquae Gratinae was already a favorite watering-place in the year 30 B.C., when Caesar took the cure.

There is little doubt in my mind that when the Roman Emperor first arrived he found a colony of spinsters and retired army officers (from recently conquered Britain) living around this spring in popinae (which are supposed to have corresponded to our modern boarding-house), wearing waterproof togas and common-sense cothurni, with double cork soles.

The wife of another Caesar fled hither in 1814. The little inn where she passed a summer in the company of her one-eyed lover - while the fate of her husband and son was being decided at Vienna and Waterloo - is still standing, and serves as the annex of a vast new hotel.

The way in which a watering-place is "run" abroad, where tourists are regarded as godsends, to be cherished, spoiled, and despoiled, is amusingly different from the manner of our village populations when summer visitors (whom they look upon as natural enemies) appear on the scene. Abroad the entire town, together with the surrounding villages, hamlets, and farmhouses, rack their brains and devote their time to inventing new amusements for the visitor, and original ways of enticing the gold from his pocket - for, mind you, on both continents the object is the same. In Europe the rural Machiavellis have had time to learn that smiling faces and picturesque surroundings are half the battle.

Another point which is perfectly understood abroad is that a cure must be largely mental; that in consequence boredom retards recovery. So during every hour of the day and evening a different amusement is provided for those who feel inclined to be amused. At Aix, for instance, Colonne's orchestra plays under the trees at the Villa des Fleurs while you are sipping your after-luncheon coffee. At three o'clock "Guignol" performs for the youngsters. At five o'clock there is another concert in the Casino. At eight o'clock an operetta is given at the villa, and a comedy in the Casino, both ending discreetly at eleven o'clock. Once a week, as a variety, the park is illuminated and fireworks help to pass the evening.

If neither music nor Guignol tempts you, every form of trap from a four-horse break to a donkey-chair (the latter much in fashion since the English queen's visit) is standing ready in the little square. On the neighboring lake you have but to choose between a dozen kinds of boats. The hire of all these modes of conveyance being fixed by the municipality, and plainly printed in boat or carriage, extortions or discussions are impossible. If you prefer a ramble among the hills, the wily native is lying in wait for you there also. When you arrive breathless at your journey's end, a shady arbor offers shelter where you may cool off and enjoy the view. It is not by accident that a dish of freshly gathered strawberries and a bowl of milk happen to be standing near by.

When bicycling around the lake you begin to feel how nice a half hour's rest would be. Presto! a terrace overhanging the water appears, and a farmer's wife who proposes brewing you a cup of tea, supplementing it with butter and bread of her own making. Weak human nature cannot withstand such blandishments. You find yourself becoming fond of the people and their smiling ways, returning again and again to shores where you are made so welcome. The fact that "business" is at the bottom of all this in no way interferes with one's enjoyment. On the contrary, to a practical mind it is refreshing to see how much can be made of a little, and what a fund of profit and pleasure can be extracted from small things, if one goes to work in the right way.

The trick can doubtless be overdone: at moments one feels the little game is worked a bit too openly. The other evening, for instance, when we entered the dining-room of our hotel and found it decorated with flags and flowers, because, forsooth, it was the birthday of "Victoria R. and I.," when champagne was offered at dessert and the band played "God Save the Queen," while the English solemnly stood up in their places, it did seem as if the proprietor was poking fun at his guests in a sly way.

I was apparently the only person, however, who felt this. The English were much flattered by the attention, so I snubbed myself with the reflection that if the date had been July 4, I doubtless should have considered the flags and music most a propos.

There are also moments when the vivid picture-squeness of this place comes near to palling on one. Its beauty is so suspiciously like a set scene that it gives the impression of having been arranged by some clever decorator with an eye to effect only.

One is continually reminded of that inimitable chapter in Daudet's Tartarin sur les Alpes, when the hero discovers that all Switzerland is one enormous humbug, run to attract tourists; that the cataracts are "faked," and avalanches arranged beforehand to enliven a dull season. Can anything be more delicious than the disillusion of Tartarin and his friends, just back from a perilous chamois hunt, on discovering that the animal they had exhausted themselves in following all day across the mountains, was being refreshed with hot wine in the kitchen of the hotel by its peasant owner?

When one visits the theatrical abbey across the lake and inspects the too picturesque tombs of Savoy's sovereigns, or walks in the wonderful old garden, with its intermittent spring, the suspicion occurs, in spite of one's self, that the whole scene will be folded up at sunset and the bare-footed "brother" who is showing us around with so much unction will, after our departure, hurry into another costume, and appear later as one of the happy peasants who are singing and drinking in front of that absurdly operatic little inn you pass on the drive home.

There is a certain pink cottage, with a thatched roof

and overhanging vines, about which I have serious doubts, and fully expect some day to see Columbine appear on that pistache-green balcony (where the magpie is hanging in a wicker cage), and, taking Arlequin's hand, disappear into the water-butt while Clown does a header over the half-door, and the cottage itself turns into a gilded coach, with Columbine kissing her hand from the window.

A problem which our intelligent people have not yet set themselves to solve, is being worked out abroad. The little cities of Europe have discovered that prosperity comes with the tourist, that with increased facilities of communication the township which expends the most in money and brains in attracting rich travellers to its gates is the place that will grow and prosper. It is a simple lesson, and one that I would gladly see our American watering-places learn and apply.

CHAPTER 24

THE BETTER PART

As I watch, year after year, the flowers of our aristocratic hothouses blooming behind the glass partitions of their conservatories, tended always by the same gardeners, admired by the same amateurs, and then, for the most part, withering unplucked on their virgin stems, I wonder if the wild flowers appreciate the good luck that allows them to taste the storm and the sunshine untrammelled and disperse perfume according to their own sweet will.

To drop a cumbersome metaphor, there is not the shadow of a doubt that the tamest and most monotonous lives in this country are those led by the women in our "exclusive" sets, for the good reason that they are surrounded by all the trammels of European society without enjoying any of its benefits, and live in an atmosphere that takes the taste out of existence too soon.

Girls abroad are kept away from the "world" because their social life only commences after marriage. In America, on the contrary, a woman is laid more or less on the shelf the day she becomes a wife, so that if she has not made hay while her maiden sunshine lasted, the chances are she will have but meagrely furnished lofts; and how, I ask, is a girl to harvest always in the same field?

When in this country, a properly brought up young aristocrat is presented by her mamma to an admiring circle of friends, she is quite a blasee person. The dancing classes she has attended for a couple of years before her debut (that she might know the right set of youths and maidens) have taken the bloom off her entrance into the world. She and her friends have already talked over the "men" of their circle, and decided, with a sigh, that there were matches going about. A juvenile Newporter was recently overheard deploring (to a friend of fifteen summers), "By the time we come out there will only be two matches in the market," meaning, of course, millionnaires who could provide their brides with country and city homes, yachts, and the other appurtenances of a brilliant position. Now, the unfortunate part of the affair is, that such a worldly-minded maiden will in good time be obliged to make her debut, dine, and dance through a dozen seasons without making a new acquaintance. Her migrations from town to seashore, or from one country house to another, will be but changes of scene: the actors will remain always the same. When she dines out, she can, if she cares to take the trouble, make a fair guess as to who the guests will be before she starts, for each entertainment is but a new shuffle of the too well-known pack. She is morally certain of being taken in to dinner by one of fifty men whom she has known since her childhood, and has met on an average twice a week since she was eighteen.

Of foreigners such a girl sees little beyond a stray diplomatist or two, in search of a fortune, and her glimpses of Paris society are obtained from the windows of a hotel on the Place Vendome. In London or Rome she may be presented in a few international salons, but as she finds it difficult to make her new acquaintances understand what an exalted position she occupies at home, the chances are that pique at seeing some Daisy Miller attract all the attention will drive my lady back to the city where she is known and appreciated, nothing being more difficult for an American "swell" than explaining to the uninitiated in what way her position differs from that of the rest of her compatriots.

When I see the bevies of highly educated and attractive girls who make their bows each season, I ask myself in wonder, "Who, in the name of goodness, are they to marry?"

In the very circle where so much stress is laid on a girl's establishing herself brilliantly, the fewest possible husbands are to be found. Yet, limited as such a girl's choice is, she will sooner remain single than accept a husband out of her set. She has a perfectly distinct idea of what she wants, and has lived so long in the atmosphere of wealth that existence without footmen and male cooks, horses and French clothes, appears to her impossible. Such large proportions do these details assume in her mind that each year the husband himself becomes of less importance, and what he can provide the essential point.

If an outsider is sufficiently rich, my lady may consent to unite her destinies to his, hoping to get him absorbed into her own world.

It is pathetic, considering the restricted number of eligible men going about, to see the trouble and expense that parents take to keep their daughters en evidence. When one reflects on the number of people who are disturbed when such a girl dines out, the horses and men and women who are kept up to convey her home, the time it has taken her to dress, the cost of the toilet itself, and then see the man to whom she will be consigned for the evening, - some bored man about town who has probably taken her mother in to dinner twenty years before, and will not trouble himself to talk with his neighbor, or a schoolboy, breaking in his first dress suit, - when one realizes that for many maidens this goes on night after night and season after season, it seems incredible that they should have the courage, or think it worth their while to keep up the game.

The logical result of turning eternally in the same circle is that nine times out of ten the men who marry choose girls out of their own set, some pretty stranger who has burst on their jaded vision with all the charm of the unknown. A conventional society maiden who has not been fortunate enough to meet and marry a man she loves, or whose fortune tempts her, during the first season or two that she is "out," will in all probability go on revolving in an ever-narrowing circle until she becomes stationary in its centre.

In comparison with such an existence the life of the average "summer girl" is one long frolic, as varied as that of her aristocratic sister is monotonous. Each spring she has the excitement of selecting a new battle-ground for her manoeuvres, for in the circle in which she moves, parents leave such details to their children. Once installed in the hotel of her choice, mademoiselle proceeds to make the acquaintance of an entirely new set of friends, delightful youths just arrived, and bent on making the most of their brief holidays, with whom her code of etiquette allows her to sail all day, and pass uncounted evening hours in remote corners of piazza or beach.

As the words "position" and "set" have no meaning to her young ears, and no one has ever preached to her the importance of improving her social standing, the acquaintances that chance throws in her path are accepted without question if they happen to be good-looking and amusing. She has no prejudice as to standing, and if her supply of partners runs short, she will dance and flirt with the clerk from the desk in perfect good humor - in fact, she stands rather in awe of that functionary, and admires the "English" cut of his clothes and his Eastern swagger. A large hotel is her dream of luxury, and a couple of simultaneous flirtations her ideal of bliss. No long evenings of cruel boredom, in order to be seen at smart houses, will cloud the maiden's career, no agonized anticipation of retiring partnerless from cotillion or supper will disturb her pleasure.

In the city she hails from, everybody she knows lives in about the same style. Some are said to be wealthier than others, but nothing in their way of life betrays the fact; the art of knowing how to enjoy wealth being but little understood outside of our one or two great cities. She has that tranquil sense of being the social equal of the people she meets, the absence of which makes the snob's life a burden.

During her summers away from home our "young friend" will meet other girls of her age, and form friendships that result in mutual visiting during the ensuing winter, when she will continue to add more new names to the long list of her admirers, until one fine morning she writes home to her delighted parents that she has found the right man at last, and engaged herself to him.

Never having penetrated to those sacred centres where birth and wealth are considered all-important, and ignoring the supreme importance of living in one set, the plan of life that such a woman lays out for herself is exceedingly simple. She will coquette and dance and dream her pleasant dream until Prince Charming, who is to awaken her to a new life, comes and kisses away the dew of girlhood and leads his bride out into the work-a-day world. The simple surroundings and ambitions of her youth will make it easy for this wife to follow the man of her choice, if necessary, to the remote village where he is directing a factory or to the mining camp where the foundations of a fortune lie. Life is full of delicious possibilities for her. Men who are forced to make their way in youth often turn out to be those who make "history" later, and a bride who has not become prematurely blasee to all the luxuries or pleasures of existence will know the greatest happiness that can come into a woman's life, that of rising at her husband's side, step by step, enjoying his triumphs as she shared his poverty.

CHAPTER 25

LA COMEDIE FRANCAISE A ORANGE

Idling up through the south of France, in company with a passionate lover of that fair land, we learned on arriving at Lyons, that the actors of the Comedie Francaise were to pass through there the next day, en route for Orange, where a series of fetes had been arranged by "Les Felibres." This society, composed of the writers and poets of Provence, have the preservation of the Roman theatre at Orange (perhaps the most perfect specimen of classical theatrical architecture in existence) profoundly at heart, their hope being to restore some of its pristine beauty to the ruin, and give from time to time performances of the Greek masterpieces on its disused stage.

The money obtained by these representations will be spent in the restoration of the theatre, and it is expected in time to make Orange the centre of classic drama, as Beyreuth is that of Wagnerian music.

At Lyons, the cortege was to leave the Paris train and take boats down the Rhone, to their destination. Their programme was so tempting that the offer of places in one of the craft was enough to lure us away from our prearranged route.

By eight o'clock the following morning, we were on foot, as was apparently the entire city. A cannon fired from Fort Lamothe gave the signal of our start. The river, covered with a thousand gayly decorated craft, glinted and glittered in the morning light. It world be difficult to forget that scene, - the banks of the Rhone were lined with the rural population, who had come miles in every direction to acclaim the passage of their poets.

Everywhere along our route the houses were gayly decorated and arches of flowers had been erected. We float past Vienne, a city once governed by Pontius Pilate, and Tournon, with its feudal chateau, blue in the distance, then Saint Peray, on a verdant vine-clad slope. As we pass under the bridge at Montelimar, an avalanche of flowers descends on us from above.

The rapid current of the river soon brings our flotilla opposite Vivier, whose Gothic cathedral bathes its feet in the Rhone. Saint Esprit and its antique bridge appear next on the horizon. Tradition asserts that the Holy Spirit, disguised as a stone mason, directed its construction; there were thirteen workmen each day, but at sunset, when the men gathered to be paid, but twelve could be counted.

Here the mayor and the municipal council were to have received us and delivered an address, but were not on hand. We could see the tardy cortege hastening towards the bridge as we shot away down stream.

On nearing Orange, the banks and quays of the river are alive with people. The high road, parallel with the stream, is alive with a many-colored throng. On all sides one hears the language of Mistral, and recognizes the music of Mireille sung by these pilgrims to an artistic Mecca, where a miracle is to be performed - and classic art called forth from its winding-sheet.

The population of a whole region is astir under the ardent Provencal sun, to witness a resurrection of the Drama in the historic valley of the Rhone, through whose channel the civilization and art and culture of the old world floated up into Europe to the ceaseless cry of the cigales.

Chateaurenard! our water journey is ended. Through the leafy avenues that lead to Orange, we see the arch of Marius and the gigantic proscenium of the theatre, rising above the roofs of the little city.

So few of our compatriots linger in the south of France after the spring has set in, or wander in the by-ways of that inexhaustible country, that a word about the representations at Orange may be of interest, and perchance create a desire to see the masterpieces of classic drama (the common inheritance of all civilized races) revived with us, and our stage put to its legitimate use, cultivating and elevating the taste of the people.

One would so gladly see a little of the money that is generously given for music used to revive in America a love for the classic drama.

We are certainly not inferior to our neighbors in culture or appreciation, and yet such a performance as I witnessed at Orange (laying aside the enchantment lent by the surroundings) would not be possible here. Why? But to return to my narrative.

The sun is setting as we toil, ticket in hand, up the Roman stairway to the upper rows of seats; far below the local gendarmerie who mostly understand their orders backwards are struggling with the throng, whose entrance they are apparently obstructing by every means in their power. Once seated, and having a wait of an hour before us, we amused ourselves watching the crowd filling in every corner of the vast building, like a rising tide of multi-colored water.

We had purposely chosen places on the highest and most remote benches, to test the vaunted acoustic qualities of the auditorium, and to obtain a view of the half-circle of humanity, the gigantic wall back of the stage, and the surrounding country.

As day softened into twilight, and twilight deepened into a luminous Southern night; the effect was incomparable. The belfries and roofs of mediaeval Orange rose in the clear air, overtopping the half ruined theatre in many places. The arch of Marius gleamed white against the surrounding hills, themselves violet and purple in the sunset, their shadow broken here and there by the outline of a crumbling chateau or the lights of a village.

Behind us the sentries paced along the wall, wrapped in their dark cloaks; and over all the scene, one snowtopped peak rose white on the horizon, like some classic virgin assisting at an Olympian solemnity.

On the stage, partly cleared of the debris of fifteen hundred years, trees had been left where they had grown, among fallen columns, fragments of capital and statue; near the front a superb rose-laurel recalled the Attic shores. To the right, wild grasses and herbs alternated with thick shrubbery, among which Orestes hid later, during the lamentations of his sister. To the left a gigantic fig-tree, growing again the dark wall, threw its branches far out over the stage.

It was from behind its foliage that "Gaul," "Provence," and "France," personated by three actresses of the "Francais," advanced to salute Apollo, seated on his rustic throne, in the prologue which began the performance.

Since midday the weather had been threatening. At seven o'clock there was almost a shower - a moment of terrible anxiety. What a misfortune if it should rain, just as the actors were to appear, here, where it had not rained for nearly four months! My right-hand neighbor, a citizen of Beaucaire, assures me, "It will be nothing, only a strong 'mistral' for to-morrow." An electrician is putting the finishing touches to his arrangements. He tries vainly to concentrate some light on the box where the committee is to sit, which is screened by a bit of crumbling wall, but finally gives it up.

Suddenly the bugles sound; the orchestra rings out the Marseillaise; it is eight o'clock. The sky is wild and threatening. An unseen hand strikes the three traditional blows. The Faun Lybrian slips down from a branch of a great elm, and throws himself on the steps that later are to represent the entrance to the palace of Agamemnon, and commences the prologue (an invocation to Apollo), in the midst of such confusion that we hear hardly a word. Little by little, however, the crowd quiets down, and I catch Louis Gallet's fine lines, marvellously phrased by Mesdames Bartet, Dudlay, Moreno, and the handsome Fenoux as Apollo.

The real interest of the public is only aroused, however, when The Erynnies begins. This powerful adaptation from the tragedy of AEschylus is the chef d'oeuvre of Leconte de Lisle. The silence is now complete. One feels in the air that the moment so long and so anxiously awaited has come, that a great event is about to take place. Every eye is fixed on the stage, waiting to see what will appear from behind the dark arches of the proscenium. A faint, plaintive strain of music floats out on the silence. Demons crawl among the leafy shadows. Not a light is visible, yet the centre of the stage is in strong relief, shading off into a thousand fantastic shadows. The audience sits in complete darkness. Then we see the people of Argos, winding toward us from among the trees, lamenting, as they have done each day for ten years, the long absence of their sons and their king. The old men no longer dare to consult the oracles, fearing to learn that all is lost. The beauty of this lament roused the first murmur of applause, each word, each syllable, chiming out across that vast semicircle with a clearness and an effect impossible to describe.

Now it is the sentinel, who from his watch-tower has caught the first glimpse of the returning army. We hear him dashing like a torrent down the turret stair; at the doorway, his garments blown by the wind, his body bending forward in a splendid pose of joy and exultation, he announces in a voice of thunder the arrival of the king.

So completely are the twenty thousand spectators under the spell of the drama that at this news one can feel a thrill pass over the throng, whom the splendid verses hold palpitating under their charm, awaiting only the end of the tirade to break into applause.

From that moment the performance is one long triumph. Clytemnestra (Madame Lerou) comes with her suite to receive the king (Mounet-Sully), the conqueror! I never realized before all the perfection that training can give the speaking voice. Each syllable seemed to ring out with a bell-like clearness. As she gradually rose in the last act to the scene with Orestes, I understood the use of the great wall behind the actors. It increased the power of the voices and lent them a sonority difficult to believe. The effect was over-whelming when, unable to escape death, Clytemnestra cries out her horrible imprecations.

Mounet-Sully surpassed himself. Paul Mounet gave us the complete illusion of a monster thirsting for blood, even his mother's! When striking her as she struck his father, he answers her despairing query, "Thou wouldst not slay thy mother?" "Woman, thou hast ceased to be a mother!" Dudlay (as Cassandra) reaches a splendid climax when she prophesies the misfortune hanging over her family, which she is powerless to avert.

It is impossible in feeble prose to give any idea of the impression those lines produce in the stupendous theatre, packed to its utmost limits - the wild night, with a storm in the air, a stage which seems like a clearing in some forest inhabited by Titans, the terrible tragedy of AEschylus following the graceful fete of Apollo.

After the unavoidable confusion at the beginning, the vast audience listen in profound silence to an expression of pure art. They are no longer actors we hear, but demi-gods. With voices of the storm, possessed by some divine afflatus, thundering out verses of fire - carried out of themselves in a whirlwind of passion, like antique prophets and Sibyls foretelling the misfortunes of the world!

That night will remain immutably fixed in my memory, if I live to be as old as the theatre itself. We were so moved, my companion and I, and had seen the crowd so moved, that fearing to efface the impression if we returned the second night to see Antigone, we came quietly away, pondering over it all, and realizing once again that a thing of beauty is a source of eternal delight.

CHAPTER 26

PRE-PALATIAL NEWPORT

The historic Ocean House of Newport is a ruin. Flames have laid low the unsightly structure that was at one time the best-known hotel in America. Its fifty-odd years of existence, as well as its day, are over. Having served a purpose, it has departed, together with the generation and habits of life that produced it, into the limbo where old houses, old customs, and super-annuated ideas survive, - the memory of the few who like to recall other days and wander from time to time in a reconstructed past.

There was a certain appropriateness in the manner of its taking off. The proud old structure had doubtless heard projects of rebuilding discussed by its owners (who for some years had been threatening to tear it down); wounded doubtless by unflattering truths, the hotel decided that if its days were numbered, an exit worthy of a leading role was at least possible. "Pull me down, indeed! That is all very well for ordinary hostleries, but from an establishment of my pretensions, that has received the aristocracy of the country, and countless foreign swells, something more is expected!"

So it turned the matter over and debated within its

shaky old brain (Mrs. Skewton fashion) what would be the most becoming and effective way of retiring from the social whirl. Balls have been overdone; people are no longer tempted by receptions; a banquet was out of the question. Suddenly the wily building hit on an idea. "I'll give them a feu d'artifice. There hasn't been a first-class fire here since I burned myself down fifty-three years ago! That kind of entertainment hasn't been run into the ground like everything else in these degenerate days! I'll do it in the best and most complete way, and give Newport something to talk about, whenever my name shall be mentioned in the future!"

Daudet, in his L'Immortel, shows us how some people are born lucky. His "Loisel of the Institute," although an insignificant and commonplace man, succeeded all through life in keeping himself before the public, and getting talked about as a celebrity. He even arranged (to the disgust and envy of his rivals) to die during a week when no event of importance was occupying public attention. In consequence, reporters, being short of "copy," owing to a dearth of murders and "first nights," seized on this demise and made his funeral an event.

The truth is, the Ocean House had lived so long in an atmosphere of ostentatious worldliness that, like many residents of the summer city, it had come to take itself and its "position" seriously, and imagine that the eyes of the country were fixed upon and expected something of it.

The air of Newport has always proved fatal to big hotels. One after another they have appeared and failed, the Ocean House alone dragging out a forlorn existence. As the flames worked their will and the careless crowd enjoyed the spectacle, one could not help feeling a vague regret for the old place, more for what it represented than for any intrinsic value of its own. Without greatly stretching a point it might be taken to represent a social condition, a phase, as it were, in our development. In a certain obscure way, it was an epoch-marking structure. Its building closed the era of primitive Newport, its decline corresponded with the end of the pre-palatial period - an era extending from 1845 to 1885.

During forty years Newport had a unique existence, unknown to the rest of America, and destined to have a lasting influence on her ways, an existence now as completely forgotten as the earlier boarding-house matinee dansante time. {1} The sixties, seventies, and eighties in Newport were pleasant years that many of us regret in spite of modern progress. Simple, inexpensive days, when people dined at three (looking on the newly introduced six o'clock dinners as an English innovation and modern "frill"), and "high-teaed" together dyspeptically off "sally lunns" and "preserves," washed down by coffee and chocolate, which it was the toilsome duty of a hostess to dispense from a silver-laden tray; days when "rockaways" drawn by lean, long-tailed horses and driven by mustached darkies were, if not the rule, far from being an exception.

"Dutch treat" picnics, another archaic amusement, flourished then, directed by a famous organizer at his farm, each guest being told what share of the eatables it was his duty to provide, an edict from which there was no appeal.

Sport was little known then, young men passing their

afternoons tooling solemnly up and down Bellevue Avenue in top-hats and black frock-coats under the burning August sun.

This was the epoch when the Town and Country Club was young and full of vigor. We met at each other's houses or at historic sites to hear papers read on serious subjects. One particular afternoon is vivid in my memory. We had all driven out to a point on the shore beyond the Third Beach, where the Norsemen were supposed to have landed during their apocryphal visit to this continent. It had been a hot drive, but when we stopped, a keen wind was blowing in from the sea. During a pause in the prolix address that followed, a coachman's voice was heard to mutter, "If he jaws much longer all the horses will be foundered," which brought the learned address to an ignominious and hasty termination.

Newport during the pre-palatial era affected culture, and a whiff of Boston pervaded the air, much of which was tiresome, yet with an under-current of charm and refinement. Those who had the privilege of knowing Mrs. Julia Ward Howe, will remember the pleasant "teas" and sparkling conversation she offered her guests in the unpretending cottage where the beauty of the daughter was as brilliant as the mother's wit.

Two estates on Bellevue Avenue are now without the hostesses who, in those days, showed the world what great ladies America could produce. It was the foreign-born husband of one of these women who gave Newport its first lessons in luxurious living. Until then Americans had travelled abroad and seen elaborately served meals and properly appointed stables without the ambition of copying such things at home. Colonial and revolutionary state had died out, and modern extravagance had not yet appeared. In the interregnum much was neglected that might have added to the convenience and grace of life.

In France, under Louis Philippe, and in England, during Victoria's youth, taste reached an ebb tide; in neither of those countries, however, did the general standard fall so low as here. It was owing to the savoir faire of one man that Newporters and New York first saw at home what they had admired abroad, - liveried servants in sufficient numbers, dinners served a la Russe, and breeched and booted grooms on English-built traps, innovations quickly followed by his neighbors, for the most marked characteristic of the American is his ability to "catch on."

When, during the war of the secession, our Naval Academy was removed from Annapolis and installed in the empty Atlantic House (corner of Bellevue Avenue and Pelham Street), hotel life had already begun to decline; but the Ocean House, which was considered a vast enterprise at that time, inherited from the older hotels the custom of giving Saturday evening "hops," the cottagers arriving at these informal entertainments toward nine o'clock and promenading up and down the corridors or dancing in the parlor, to the admiration of a public collected to enjoy the spectacle. At eleven the doors of the dining-room opened, and a line of well-drilled darkies passed ices and lemonade. By half-past eleven (the hour at which we now arrive at a dance) every one was at home and abed.

One remembers with a shudder the military manoeuvres that attended hotel meals in those days, the marching and countermarching, your dinner cooling while the head waiter reviewed his men. That idiotic custom has been abandoned, like many better and worse. Next to the American ability to catch on comes the facility with which he can drop a fad.

In this peculiarity the history of Newport has been an epitome of the country, every form of amusement being in turn taken up, run into the ground, and then abandoned. At one time it was the fashion to drive to Fort Adams of an afternoon and circle round and round the little green to the sounds of a military band; then, for no visible reason, people took to driving on the Third Beach, an inaccessible and lonely point which for two or three summers was considered the only correct promenade.

I blush to recall it, but at that time most of the turnouts were hired hacks. Next, Graves Point, on the Ocean Drive, became the popular meeting-place. Then society took to attending polo of an afternoon, a sport just introduced from India. This era corresponded with the opening of the Casino (the old reading-room dating from 1854). For several years every one crowded during hot August mornings onto the airless lawns and piazzas of the new establishment. It seems on looking back as if we must have been more fond of seeing each other in those days than we are now. To ride up and down a beach and bow filled our souls with joy, and the "cake walk" was an essential part of every ball, the guests parading in pairs round and round the room between the dances instead of sitting quietly "out." The opening promenade at the New York Charity Ball is a survival of this inane custom.

The disappearance of the Ocean House "hops" marked

the last stage in hotel life. Since then better-class watering places all over the country have slowly but surely followed Newport's lead. The closed caravan-saries of Bar Harbor and elsewhere bear silent testimony to the fact that refined Americans are at last awakening to the charms of home life during their holidays, and are discarding, as fast as finances will permit, the pernicious herding system. In consequence the hotel has ceased to be, what it undoubtedly was twenty years ago, the focus of our summer life.

Only a few charred rafters remain of the Ocean House. A few talkative old duffers like myself alone survive the day it represents. Changing social conditions have gradually placed both on the retired list. A new and palatial Newport has replaced the simpler city. Let us not waste too much time regretting the past, or be too sure that it was better than the present. It is quite possible, if the old times we are writing so fondly about should return, we might discover that the same thing was true of them as a ragged urchin asserted the other afternoon of the burning building:

"Say, Tom, did ye know there was the biggest room in the world in that hotel?"

"No; what room?"

"Room for improvement, ya!"

CHAPTER 27

SARDOU AT MARLY-LE-ROY

Near the centre of that verdant triangle formed by Saint Cloud, Versailles, and Saint Germain lies the village of Marly-le-Roy, high up on a slope above the lazy Seine - an entrancing corner of the earth, much affected formerly by French crowned heads, and by the "Sun King" in particular, who in his old age grew tired of Versailles and built here one of his many villas (the rival in its day of the Trianons), and proceeded to amuse himself therein with the same solemnity which had already made vice at Versailles more boresome than virtue elsewhere.

Two centuries and four revolutions have swept away all trace of this kingly caprice and the art treasures it contained. Alone, the marble horses of Coustou, transported later to the Champs Elysees, remain to attest the splendor of the past.

The quaint village of Marly, clustered around its church, stands, however - with the faculty that insignificant things have of remaining unchanged - as it did when the most polished court of Europe rode through it to and from the hunt. On the outskirts of this village are now two forged and gilded gateways through which the passer-by can catch a glimpse of trim avenues, fountains, and well-kept lawns.

There seems a certain poetical justice in the fact that Alexandre Dumas fils and Victorien Sardou, the two giants of modern drama, should have divided between them the inheritance of Louis XIV., its greatest patron. One of the gates is closed and moss-grown. Its owner lies in Pere-la-Chaise. At the other I ring, and am soon walking up the famous avenue bordered by colossal sphinxes presented to Sardou by the late Khedive. The big stone brutes, connected in one's mind with heat and sandy wastes, look oddly out of place here in this green wilderness - a bite, as it were, out of the forest which, under different names, lies like a mantle over the country-side.

Five minutes later I am being shown through a suite of antique salons, in the last of which sits the great playwright. How striking the likeness is to Voltaire, - the same delicate face, lit by a half cordial, half mocking smile; the same fragile body and indomitable spirit. The illusion is enhanced by our surroundings, for the mellow splendor of the room where we stand might have served as a background for the Sage of Ferney.

Wherever one looks, works of eighteenth-century art meet the eye. The walls are hung with Gobelin tapestries that fairly take one's breath away, so exquisite is their design and their preservation. They represent a marble colonnade, each column of which is wreathed with flowers and connected to its neighbor with garlands.

Between them are bits of delicate landscape, with here and there a group of figures dancing or picnicking in the shadow of tall trees or under fantastical porticos. The furniture of the room is no less marvellous than its hangings. One turns from a harpsichord of vernis-martin to the clock, a relic from Louis XIV.'s bedroom in Versailles; on to the bric-a-brac of old Saxe or Sevres in admiring wonder. My host drifts into his showman manner, irresistibly comic in this writer.

The pleasures of the collector are apparently divided into three phases, without counting the rapture of the hunt. First, the delight a true amateur takes in living among rare and beautiful things. Second, the satisfaction of showing one's treasures to less fortunate mortals, and last, but perhaps keenest of all, the pride which comes from the fact that one has been clever enough to acquire objects which other people want, at prices below their market value. Sardou evidently enjoys these three sensations vividly. That he lives with and loves his possessions is evident, and the smile with which he calls your attention to one piece after another, and mentions what they cost him, attests that the two other joys are not unknown to him. He is old enough to remember the golden age when really good things were to be picked up for modest sums, before every parvenu considered it necessary to turn his house into a museum, and factories existed for the production of "antiques" to be sold to innocent amateurs.

In calling attention to a set of carved and gilded furniture, covered in Beauvais tapestry, such as sold recently in Paris at the Valencay sale - Talleyrand collection - for sixty thousand dollars, Sardou mentions with a laugh that he got his fifteen pieces for fifteen hundred dollars, the year after the war, from an old chateau back of Cannes! One unique piece of tapestry had cost him less than one-tenth of that sum.

He discovered it in a peasant's stable under a two-foot layer of straw and earth, where it had probably been hidden a hundred years before by its owner, and then all record of it lost by his descendants.

The mention of Cannes sets Sardou off on another train of thought. His family for three generations have lived there. Before that they were Sardinian fishermen. His great-grandfather, he imagines, was driven by some tempest to the shore near Cannes and settled where he found himself. Hence the name! For in the patois of Provencal France an inhabitant of Sardinia is still called un Sardou.

The sun is off the front of the house by this time, so we migrate to a shady corner of the lawn for our aperitif, the inevitable vermouth or "bitters" which Frenchmen take at five o'clock. Here another surprise awaits the visitor, who has not realized, perhaps, to what high ground the crawling local train has brought him. At our feet, far below the lawn and shade trees that encircle the chateau, lies the Seine, twisting away toward Saint Germain, whose terrace and dismantled palace stand outlined against the sky. To our right is the plain of Saint Denis, the cathedral in its midst looking like an opera-glass on a green table. Further still to the right, as one turns the corner of the terrace, lies Paris, a white line on the horizon, broken by the mass of the Arc de Triomphe, the roof of the Opera, and the Eiffel Tower, resplendent in a fresh coat of yellow lacquer!

The ground where we stand was occupied by the feudal castle of Les Sires de Marly; although all traces of that stronghold disappeared centuries ago, the present owner of the land points out with pride that the extraordinary beauty of the trees around his house is owing to the fact that their roots reach deep down to the rich loam collected during centuries in the castle's moat.

The little chateau itself, built during the reign of Louis XIV. for the grand-veneur of the forest of Marly, is intensely French in type, - a long, low building on a stone terrace, with no trace of ornament about its white facade or on its slanting roof. Inside, all the rooms are "front," communicating with each other en suite, and open into a corridor running the length of the building at the back, which, in turn, opens on a stone court. Two lateral wings at right angles to the main building form the sides of this courtyard, and contain les communs, the kitchen, laundry, servants' rooms, and the other annexes of a large establishment. This arrangement for a summer house is for some reason neglected by our American architects. I can recall only one home in America built on this plan. It is Giraud Foster's beautiful villa at Lenox. You may visit five hundred French chateaux and not find one that differs materially from this plan. The American idea seems on the contrary to be a square house with a room in each corner, and all the servants' quarters stowed away in a basement. Cottage and palace go on reproducing that foolish and inconvenient arrangement indefinitely.

After an hour's chat over our drinks, during host has rippled on from one subject to another with the lightness of touch of a born talker, we get on to the subject of the grounds, and his plans for their improvement.

Good luck has placed in Sardou's hands an old map of the gardens as they existed in the time of Louis XV., and several prints of the chateau dating from about the same epoch have found their way into his portfolios. The grounds are, under his care, slowly resuming the appearance of former days. Old avenues reopen, statues reappear on the disused pedestals, fountains play again, and clipped hedges once more line out the terraced walks.

In order to explain how complete this work will be in time, Sardou hurries me off to inspect another part of his collection. Down past the stables, in an unused corner of the grounds, long sheds have been erected, under which is stored the debris of a dozen palaces, an assortment of eighteenth-century art that could not be duplicated even in France.

One shed shelters an entire semicircle of treillage, pure Louis XV., an exquisite example of a lost art. Columns, domes, panels, are packed away in straw awaiting resurrection in some corner hereafter to be chosen. A dozen seats in rose-colored marble from Fontainebleau are huddled together near by in company with a row of gigantic marble masques brought originally from Italy to decorate Fouquet's fountains at his chateau of Vaux in the short day of its glory. Just how this latter find is to be utilized their owner has not yet decided. The problem, however, to judge from his manner, is as important to the great playwright as the plot of his next drama.

That the blood of an antiquarian runs in Sardou's veins is evident in the subdued excitement with which he shows you his possessions - statues from Versailles, forged gates and balconies from Saint Cloud, the carved and gilded wood-work for a dozen rooms culled from the four corners of France. Like the true dramatist, he has, however, kept his finest effect for the last. In the centre of a circular rose garden near by stands, alone in its beauty, a column from the facade of the Tuileries, as perfect from base to flower-crowned capital as when Philibert Delorme's workmen laid down their tools.

Years ago Sardou befriended a young stone mason, who through this timely aid prospered, and, becoming later a rich builder, received in 1882 from the city of Paris the contract to tear down the burned ruins of the Tuileries. While inspecting the palace before beginning the work of demolition, he discovered one column that had by a curious chance escaped both the flames of the Commune and the patriotic ardor of 1793, which effaced all royal emblems from church and palace alike. Remembering his benefactor's love for antiquities with historical associations, the grateful contractor appeared one day at Marly with this column on a dray, and insisted on erecting it where it now stands, pointing out to Sardou with pride the crowned "H," of Henri Quatre, and the entwined "M. M." of Marie de Medicis, topped by the Florentine lily in the flutings of the shaft and on the capital.

A question of mine on Sardou's manner of working led to our abandoning the gardens and mounting to the top floor of the chateau, where his enormous library and collection of prints are stored in a series of little rooms or alcoves, lighted from the top and opening on a corridor which runs the length of the building. In each room stands a writing-table and a chair; around the walls from floor to ceiling and in huge portfolios are arranged his books and engravings according to their subject. The Empire alcove, for instance, contains nothing but publications and pictures relating to that epoch. Roman and Greek history have their alcoves, as have mediaeval history and the reigns of the different Louis. Nothing could well be conceived more conducive to study than this arrangement, and it makes one realize how honest was the master's reply when asked what was his favorite amusement. "Work!" answered the author.

Our conversation, as was fated, soon turned to the enormous success of Robespierre in London - a triumph that even Sardou's many brilliant victories had not yet equalled.

It is characteristic of the French disposition that neither the author nor any member of his family could summon courage to undertake the prodigious journey from Paris to London in order to see the first performance. Even Sardou's business agent, M. Roget, did not get further than Calais, where his courage gave out. "The sea was so terrible!" Both those gentlemen, however, took it quite as a matter of course that Sardou's American agent should make a three-thousand-mile journey to be present at the first night.

The fact that the French author resisted Sir Henry Irving's pressing invitations to visit him in no way indicates a lack of interest in the success of the play. I had just arrived from London, and so had to go into every detail of the performance, a rather delicate task, as I had been discouraged with the acting of both Miss Terry and Irving, who have neither of them the age, voice, nor temperament to represent either the revolutionary tyrant or the woman he betrayed. As the staging had been excellent, I enlarged on that side of the subject, but when pressed into a corner by the author, had to acknowledge that in the scene where Robespierre, alone at midnight in the Conciergerie, sees the phantoms of his victims advance from the surrounding shadows and form a menacing circle around him, Irving had used his poor voice with so little skill that there was little left for the splendid climax, when, in trying to escape from his ghastly visitors, Robespierre finds himself face to face with Marie Antoinette, and with a wild cry, half of horror, half of remorse, falls back insensible.

In spite of previous good resolutions, I must have given the author the impression that Sir Henry spoke too loud at the beginning of this scene and was in consequence inadequate at the end.

"What!" cried Sardou. "He raised his voice in that act! Why, it's a scene to be played with the soft pedal down! This is the way it should be done!" Dropping into a chair in the middle of the room my host began miming the gestures and expression of Robespierre as the phantoms (which, after all, are but the figments of an over-wrought brain) gather around him. Gradually he slipped to the floor, hiding his face with his upraised elbow, whispering and sobbing, but never raising his voice until, staggering toward the portal to escape, he meets the Queen face to face. Then the whole force of his voice came out in one awful cry that fairly froze the blood in my veins!

"What a teacher you would make!" instinctively rose to my lips as he ended.

With a careless laugh, Sardou resumed his shabby velvet cap, which had fallen to the floor, and answered: "Oh, it's nothing! I only wanted to prove to you that the scene was not a fatiguing one for the voice if played properly. I'm no actor and could not teach, but any one ought to know enough not to shout in that scene!"

This with some bitterness, as news had arrived that Irving's voice had given out the night before, and he had been replaced by his half-baked son in the title role, a change hardly calculated to increase either the box-office receipts or the success of the new drama.

Certain ominous shadows which, like Robespierre's visions, had been for some time gathering in the corners of the room warned me that the hour had come for my trip back to Paris. Declining reluctantly an invitation to take potluck with my host, I was soon in the Avenue of the Sphinx again. As we strolled along, talking of the past and its charm, a couple of men passed us, carrying a piece of furniture rolled in burlaps.

"Another acquisition?" I asked. "What epoch has tempted you this time?"

"I'm sorry you won't stop and inspect it," answered Sardou with a twinkle in his eye. "It's something I bought yesterday for my bedroom. An armchair! Pure Loubet!"

CHAPTER 28

INCONSISTENCIES

The dinner had been unusually long and the summer evening warm. During the wait before the dancing began I must have dropped asleep in the dark corner of the piazza where I had installed myself, to smoke my cigar, away from the other men and their tiresome chatter of golf and racing. Through the open window groups of women could be seen in the ball-room, and the murmur of their conversation floated out, mingling with the laughter of the men.

Suddenly, in that casual way peculiar to dreams, I found myself conversing with a solemn young Turk, standing in all the splendor of fez and stambouline beside my chair.

"Pardon, Effendi," he was murmuring. "Is this an American ball? I was asked at nine o'clock; it is now past eleven. Is there not some mistake?"

"None," I answered. "When a hostess puts nine o'clock on her card of invitation she expects her guests at eleven or half-past, and would be much embarrassed to be taken literally."

As we were speaking, our host rose. The men,

reluctantly throwing away their cigars, began to enter the ball-room through the open windows. On their approach the groups of women broke up, the men joining the girls where they sat, or inviting them out to the lantern-lit piazza, where the couples retired to dim, palm-embowered corners.

"Are you sure I have not made a mistake?" asked my interlocutor, with a faint quiver of the eyelids. "It is my intention, while travelling, to remain faithful to my harem."

I hastened to reassure him and explain that he was in an exclusive and reserved society.

"Indeed," he murmured incredulously. "When I was passing through New York last winter a lady was pointed out to me as the owner of marvellous jewels and vast wealth, but with absolutely no social position. My informant added that no well-born woman would receive her or her husband.

"It's foolish, of course, but the handsome woman with the crown on sitting in the centre of that circle, looks very like the woman I mean. Am I right?"

"It's the same lady," I answered, wearily. "You are speaking of last year. No one could be induced to call on the couple then. Now we all go to their house, and entertain them in return."

"They have doubtless done some noble action, or the reports about the husband have been proved false?"

"Nothing of the kind has taken place. She's a success, and no one asks any questions! In spite of that, you are in a society where the standard of conduct is held higher than in any country of Europe, by a race of women more virtuous, in all probability, than has yet been seen. There is not a man present," I added, "who would presume to take, or a woman who would permit, a liberty so slight even as the resting of a youth's arm across the back of her chair."

While I was speaking, an invisible orchestra began to sigh out the first passionate bars of a waltz. A dozen couples rose, the men clasping in their arms the slender matrons, whose smiling faces sank to their partners' shoulders. A blond mustache brushed the forehead of a girl as she swept by us to the rhythm of the music, and other cheeks seemed about to touch as couples glided on in unison.

The sleepy Oriental eyes of my new acquaintance opened wide with astonishment.

"This, you must understand," I continued, hastily, "is quite another matter. Those people are waltzing. It is considered perfectly proper, when the musicians over there play certain measures, for men to take apparent liberties. Our women are infinitely self-respecting, and a man who put his arm around a woman (in public) while a different measure was being played, or when there was no music, would be ostracized from polite society."

"I am beginning to understand," replied the Turk. "The husbands and brothers of these women guard them very carefully. Those men I see out there in the dark are doubtless with their wives and sisters, protecting them from the advances of other men. Am I right?"

"Of course you're not right," I snapped out, beginning to lose my temper at his obtuseness. "No husband would dream of talking to his wife in public, or of sitting with her in a corner. Every one would be laughing at them. Nor could a sister be induced to remain away from the ball-room with her brother. Those girls are 'sitting out' with young men they like, indulging in a little innocent flirtation."

"What is that?" he asked. "Flirtation?"

"An American custom rather difficult to explain. It may, however, be roughly defined as the art of leading a man a long way on the road to - nowhere!"

"Women flirt with friends or acquaintances, never with members of their family?"

"The husbands are those dejected individuals wandering aimlessly about over there like lost souls. They are mostly rich men, who, having married beautiful girls for love, wear themselves out maintaining elaborate and costly establishments for them. In return for his labor a husband, however, enjoys but little of his wife's society, for a really fashionable woman can rarely be induced to go home until she has collapsed with fatigue. In consequence, she contributes little but 'nerves' and temper to the household. Her sweetest smiles, like her freshest toilets, are kept for the public. The husband is the last person considered in an American household. If you doubt what I say, look behind you. There is a newly married man speaking with his wife, and trying to persuade her to leave before the cotillion begins. Notice his apologetic air! He knows he is interrupting a tender conversation and taking an unwarrantable liberty. Nothing short of

Eliot Gregory

extreme fatigue would drive him to such an extremity. The poor millionnaire has hardly left his desk in Wall Street during the week, and only arrived this evening in time to dress for dinner. He would give a fair slice of his income for a night's rest. See! He has failed, and is lighting another cigar, preparing, with a sigh, for a long wait. It will be three before my lady is ready to leave."

After a silence of some minutes, during which he appeared to be turning these remarks over in his mind, the young Oriental resumed: "The single men who absorb so much of your women's time and attention are doubtless the most distinguished of the nation, - writers, poets, and statesmen?"

I was obliged to confess that this was not the case; that, on the contrary, the dancing bachelors were for the most part impecunious youths of absolutely no importance, asked by the hostess to fill in, and so lightly considered that a woman did not always recognize in the street her guests of the evening before.

At this moment my neighbor's expression changed from bewilderment to admiration, as a young and very lovely matron threw herself, panting, into a low chair at his side. Her decollete was so daring that the doubts of half an hour before were evidently rising afresh in his mind. Hastily resuming my task of mentor, I explained that a decollete corsage was an absolute rule for evening gatherings. A woman who appeared in a high bodice or with her neck veiled would be considered lacking in politeness to her hostess as much if she wore a bonnet.

"With us, women go into the world to shine and charm.

It is only natural they should use all the weapons nature has given them."

"Very good!" exclaimed the astonished Ottoman. "But where will all this end? You began by allowing your women to appear in public with their faces unveiled, then you suppressed the fichu and the collarette, and now you rob them of half their corsage. Where, O Allah, will you stop?"

"Ah!" I answered, laughing, "the tendency of civilization is to simplify; many things may yet disappear."

"I understand perfectly. You have no prejudice against women wearing in public toilets that we consider fitted only for strict intimacy. In that case your ladies may walk about the streets in these costumes?"

"Not at all!" I cried. "It would provoke a scandal if a woman were to be seen during the daytime in such attire, either at home or abroad. The police and the law courts would interfere. Evening dress is intended only for reunions in private houses, or at most, to be worn at entertainments where the company is carefully selected and the men asked from lists prepared by the ladies themselves. No lady would wear a ball costume or her jewels in a building where the general public was admitted. In London great ladies dine at restaurants in full evening dress, but we Americans, like the French, consider that vulgar."

"Yet, last winter," he said, "when passing through New York, I went to a great theatre, where there were an orchestra and many singing people. Were not those respectable women I saw in the boxes? There were no moucharabies to screen them from the eyes of the public. Were all the men in that building asked by special invitation? That could hardly be possible, for I paid an entrance fee at the door. From where I sat I could see that, as each lady entered her box, opera-glasses were fixed on her, and her 'points,' as you say, discussed by the crowd of men in the corridors, who, apparently, belonged to quite the middle class."

"My poor, innocent Padischa, you do not understand at all. That was the opera, which makes all the difference. The husbands of those women pay enormous prices, expressly that their wives may exhibit themselves in public, decked in jewels and suggestive toilets. You could buy a whole harem of fair Circassians for what one of those little square boxes costs. A lady whose entrance caused no sensation would feel bitterly disappointed. As a rule, she knows little about music, and cares still less, unless some singer is performing who is paid a fabulous price, which gives his notes a peculiar charm. With us most things are valued by the money they have cost. Ladies attend the opera simply and solely to see their friends and be admired.

"It grieves me to see that you are forming a poor opinion of our woman kind, for they are more charming and modest than any foreign women. A girl or matron who exhibits more of her shoulders than you, with your Eastern ideas, think quite proper, would sooner expire than show an inch above her ankle. We have our way of being modest as well as you, and that is one of our strongest prejudices."

"Now I know you are joking," he replied, with a slight show of temper, "or trying to mystify me, for only this morning I was on the beach watching the bathing, and I saw a number of ladies in quite short skirts - up to their knees, in fact - with the thinnest covering on their shapely extremities. Were those women above suspicion?"

"Absolutely," I assured him, feeling inclined to tear my hair at such stupidity. "Can't you see the difference? That was in daylight. Our customs allow a woman to show her feet, and even a little more, in the morning. It would be considered the acme of indecency to let those beauties be seen at a ball. The law allows a woman to uncover her neck and shoulders at a ball, but she would be arrested if she appeared decollete on the beach of a morning."

A long silence followed, broken only by the music and laughter from the ball-room. I could see my dazed Mohammedan remove his fez and pass an agitated hand through his dark hair; then he turned, and saluting me gravely, murmured:

"It is very kind of you to have taken so much trouble with me. I do not doubt that what you have said is full of the wisdom and consistency of a new civilization, which I fail to appreciate." Then, with a sigh, he added: "It will be better for me to return to my own country, where there are fewer exceptions to rules."

With a profound salaam the gentle youth disappeared into the surrounding darkness, leaving me rubbing my eyes and asking myself if, after all, the dreamland Oriental was not about right. Custom makes many inconsistencies appear so logical that they no longer cause us either surprise or emotion. But can we explain them?

CHAPTER 29

MODERN "CADETS DE GASCOGNE"

After witnessing the performance given by the Comedie Francaise in the antique theatre at Orange, we determined - my companion and I - if ever another opportunity of the kind offered, to attend, be the material difficulties what they might.

The theatrical "stars" in their courses proved favorable to the accomplishment of this vow. Before the year ended it was whispered to us that the "Cadets de Gascogne" were planning a tram through the Cevennes Mountains and their native Languedoc - a sort of lay pilgrimage to famous historic and literary shrines, a voyage to be enlivened by much crowning of busts and reciting of verses in the open air, and incidentally, by the eating of Gascony dishes and the degustation of delicate local wines; the whole to culminate with a representation in the arena at Beziers of Dejanire, Louis Gallet's and Saint-Saens's latest work, under the personal supervision of those two masters.

A tempting programme, was it not, in these days of cockney tours and "Cook" couriers? At any rate, one that we, with plenty of time on our hands and a weakness for out-of-the-way corners and untrodden paths, found it impossible to resist.

Rostand, in Cyrano de Bergerac, has shown us the "Cadets" of Moliere's time, a fighting, rhyming, devil-may-care band, who wore their hearts on their sleeves and chips on their stalwart shoulders; much such a brotherhood, in short, as we love to imagine that Shakespeare, Kit Marlowe, Greene, and their intimates formed when they met at the "Ship" to celebrate a success or drink a health to the drama.

The men who compose the present society (which has now for many years borne a name only recently made famous by M. Rostand's genius) come delightfully near realizing the happy conditions of other days, and - less the fighting - form as joyous and picturesque a company as their historic elders. They are for the most part Southern-born youths, whose interests and ambitions centre around the stage, devotees at the altar of Melpomene, ardent lovers of letters and kindred arts, and proud of the debt that literary France owes to Gascony.

It is the pleasant custom of this coterie to meet on winter evenings in unfrequented cafes, transformed by them for the time into clubs, where they recite new-made verses, discuss books and plays, enunciate paradoxes that make the very waiters shudder, and, between their "bocks," plan vast revolutions in the world of literature.

As the pursuit of "letters" is, if anything, less lucrative in France than in other countries, the question of next day's dinner is also much discussed among these budding Molieres, who are often forced to learn early in their careers, when meals have been meagre, to satisfy themselves with rich rhymes and drink their fill of flowing verse.

From time to time older and more successful members of the corporation stray back into the circle, laying aside their laurel crowns and Olympian pose, in the society of the new-comers to Bohemia. These honorary members enjoy nothing more when occasion offers than to escape from the toils of greatness and join the "Cadets" in their summer journeys to and fro in France, trips which are made to combine the pleasures of an outing with the aims of a literary campaign. It was an invitation to join one of these tramps that tempted my friend and me away from Paris at the season when that city is at its best. Being unable, on account of other engagements, to start with the cohort from the capital, we made a dash for it and caught them up at Carcassonne during the fetes that the little Languedoc city was offering to its guests.

After having seen Aigues Mortes, it was difficult to believe that any other place in Europe could suggest more vividly the days of military feudalism. St. Louis's tiny city is, however, surpassed by Carcassonne!

Thanks to twenty years of studious restoration by Viollet le Duc, this antique jewel shines in its setting of slope and plain as perfect to-day (seen from the distance) as when the Crusaders started from its crenelated gates for the conquest of the Holy Sepulchre. The acropolis of Carcassonne is crowned with Gothic battlements, the golden polygon of whose walls, rising from Roman foundations and layers of ruddy Visigoth brick to the stately marvel of its fifty towers, forms a whole that few can view unmoved.

We found the Cadets lunching on the platform of the great western keep, while a historic pageant organized in their honor was winding through the steep mediaeval streets - a cavalcade of archers, men at arms, and many-colored troubadours, who, after effecting a triumphal entrance to the town over lowered drawbridges, mounted to unfurl their banner on our tower. As the gaudy standard unfolded on the evening air, Mounet-Sully's incomparable voice breathed the very soul of the "Burgraves" across the silent plain and down through the echoing corridors below. While we were still under the impression of the stirring lines, he changed his key and whispered:-

> *Le soir tombe. . . . L'heure douce*
> *Qui s'eloigne sans secousse,*
> *Pose a peine sur la mousse*
> *Ses pieds.*
> *Un jour indecis persiste,*
> *Et le crepuscule triste*
> *Ouvre ses yeux d'amethyste*
> *Mouilles.*

Night came on ere the singing and reciting ended, a balmy Southern evening, lit by a thousand fires from tower and battlement and moat, the old walls glowing red against the violet sky.

Picture this scene to yourself, reader mine, and you will understand the enthusiasm of the artists and writers in our clan. It needed but little imagination then to reconstruct the past and fancy one's self back in the days when the "Trancavel" held this city against the world.

Sleep that night was filled with a strange phantas-magoria of crenelated chateaux and armored knights, until the bright Provencal sunlight and the call for a hurried departure dispelled such illusions. By noon we were far away from Carcassonne, mounting the rocky slopes of the Cevennes amid a wild and noble landscape; the towering cliffs of the "Causses," zebraed by zig-zag paths, lay below us, disclosing glimpses of fertile valley and vine-engarlanded plain.

One asks one's self in wonder why these enchanting regions are so unknown. En route our companions were like children fresh from school, taking haphazard meals at the local inns and clambering gayly into any conveyance that came to hand. As our way led us through the Cevennes country, another charm gradually stole over the senses.

"I imagine that Citheron must look like this," murmured Catulle Mendes, as we stood looking down from a sun-baked eminence, "with the Gulf of Corinth there where you see that gleam of water." As he spoke he began declaiming the passage from Sophocles's OEdipus the King descriptive if that classic scene.

Two thousand feet below lay Ispanhac in a verdant valley, the River Tarn gleaming amid the cultivated fields like a cimeter thrown on a Turkish carpet. Our descent was an avalanche of laughing, singing "Cadets," who rolled in the fresh-cut grass and chased each other through the ripening vineyards, shouting lines from tragedies to groups of open-mouthed farm-hands, and invading the tiny inns on the road with song and tumult. As we neared our goal its entire population, headed by the cure, came out to meet us and offer the hospitality of the town.

In the market-place, one of our number, inspired by the antique solemnity of the surroundings, burst into the noble lines of Hugo's Devant Dieu, before which the awestruck population uncovered and crossed themselves, imagining, doubtless, that it was a religious ceremony.

Another scene recurs vividly to my memory. We were at St. Enimie. I had opened my window to breathe the night air after the heat and dust of the day and watch the moonlight on the quaint bridge at my feet. Suddenly from out the shadows there rose (like sounds in a dream) the exquisite tone of Sylvain's voice, alternating with the baritone of d'Esparbes. They were seated at the water's edge, intoxicated by the beauty of the scene and apparently oblivious of all else.

The next day was passed on the Tarn, our ten little boats following each other single file on the narrow river, winding around the feet of mighty cliffs, or wandering out into sunny pasture lands where solitary peasants, interrupted in their labors, listened in astonishment to the chorus thundered from the passing boats, and waved us a welcome as we moved by.

Space is lacking to give more than a suggestion of those days, passed in every known conveyance from the antique diligence to the hissing trolley, in company with men who seemed to have left their cares and their years behind them in Paris.

Our last stop before arriving at Beziers was at La Case, where luncheon was served in the great hall of the chateau. Armand Sylvestre presided at the repast; his verses alternated with the singings of Emma Calve, who had come from her neighboring chateau to greet her old friends and compatriots, the "Cadets."

As the meal terminated, more than one among the

guests, I imagine, felt his heart heavy with the idea that to-morrow would end this pleasant ramble and send him back to the realities of life and the drudgery of daily bread-winning.

The morning of the great day dawned cloudless and cool. A laughing, many-colored throng early invaded the arena, the women's gay toilets lending it some resemblance to a parterre of fantastic flowers. Before the bell sounded its three strokes that announced the representation, over ten thousand spectators had taken their places and were studying the gigantic stage and its four thousand yards of painted canvas. In the foreground a cluster of Greek palaces and temples surround a market-place; higher up and further back the city walls, manned by costumed sentinels, rise against mountains so happily painted that their outlines blend with nature's own handiwork in the distance, - a worthy setting for a stately drama and the valiant company of actors who have travelled from the capital for this solemnity.

Three hundred hidden musicians, divided into wind and chord orchestras, accompany a chorus of two hundred executants, and furnish the music for a ballet of seventy dancers.

As the third stroke dies away, the Muse, Mademoiselle Rabuteau, enters and declaims the salutation addressed by Louis Gallet to the City of Beziers. At its conclusion the tragedy begins.

This is not the place to describe or criticise at length so new an attempt at classic restoration. The author follows the admirable fable of antiquity with a directness and simplicity worthy of his Greek model.

The story of Dejanira and Hercules is too familiar to be repeated here. The hero's infidelity and the passion of a neglected woman are related through five acts logically and forcibly, with the noble music of Saint-Saens as a background.

We watch the growing affection of the demi-god for the gentle Iole. We sympathize with jealous, desperate Dejanira when in a last attempt to gain back the love of Hercules she persuades the unsuspecting Iole to offer him a tunic steeped in Nessus's blood, which Dejanira has been told by Centaur will when warmed in the sun restore the wearer to her arms.

At the opening of the fifth act we witness the nuptial fetes. Religious dances and processions circle around the pyre laid for a marriage sacrifice. Dejanira, hidden in the throng, watches in an agony of hope for the miracle to be worked.

Hercules accepts the fatal garment from the hands of his bride and calls upon the sun-god to ignite the altars. The pyre flames, the heat warms the clinging tunic, which wraps Hercules in its folds of torture. Writhing in agony, he flings himself upon the burning pyramid, followed by Dejanira, who, in despair, sees too late that she has been but a tool in the hands of Nessus.

No feeble prose, no characters of black or white, can do justice to the closing scenes of this performance. The roar of the chorus, the thunder of the actors' voices, the impression of reality left on the breathless spectators by the open-air reality of the scene, the ardent sun, the rustling wind, the play of light and shade across the stage, the invocation of Hercules addressed to the real heavens, not to a painted firmament, combined an effect that few among that vast concourse will forget.

At the farewell banquet in the arena after the performance, Georges Leygues, the captain of the Cadets, in answer to a speech from the Prefect, replied: "You ask about our aims and purposes and speak in admiration of the enthusiasm aroused by the passage of our band!

"Our aims are to vivify the traditions and language of our native land, and the memory of a glorious ancestry, to foster the love of our little province at the same time as patriotism for the greater country. We are striving for a decentralization of art, for the elevation of the stage; but above all, we preach a gospel of gayety and healthy laughter, the science of remaining young at heart, would teach pluck and good humor in the weary struggle of existence, characteristics that have marked our countrymen through history! We have borrowed a motto from Lope de Vega (that Gascon of another race), and inscribe 'Par la langua et par l'epee' upon our banner, that these purposes may be read by the world as it runs."

CHAPTER 30

THE DINNER AND THE DRAMA

Claude Frollo, holding the first printed book he had seen in one hand, and pointing with the other to the gigantic mass of Notre Dame, dark against the sunset, prophesied "Ceci tuera cela." One might to-day paraphrase the sentence which Victor Hugo put into his archdeacon's mouth, and pointing to the elaborately appointed dinner-tables of our generation, assert that the Dinner was killing the Drama.

New York undoubtedly possesses at this moment more and better constructed theatres, in proportion to its population, than any other city on the globe, and, with the single exception of Paris, more money is probably spent at the theatre by our people than in any other metropolis. Yet curiously enough, each decade, each season widens the breach between our discriminating public and the stage. The theatre, instead of keeping abreast with the intellectual movement of our country, has for the last thirty years been slowly but steadily declining, until at this moment there is hardly a company playing in legitimate comedy, tragedy, or the classic masterpieces of our language.

In spite of the fact that we are a nation in full literary production, boasting authors who rank with the greatest of other countries, there is hardly one poet or prose-writer to-day, of recognized ability, who works for the stage, nor can we count more than one or two high-class comedies or lyric dramas of American origin.

It is not my intention here to criticise the contemporary stage, although the condition of the drama in America is so unique and so different from its situation in other countries that it might well attract the attention of inquiring minds; but rather to glance at the social causes which have produced this curious state of affairs, and the strained relations existing between our elite (here the word is used in its widest and most elevated sense) and our stage.

There can be little doubt that the deterioration in the class of plays produced at our theatres has been brought about by changes in our social conditions. The pernicious "star" system, the difficulty of keeping stock companies together, the rarity of histrionic ability among Americans are explanations which have at different times been offered to account for these phenomena. Foremost, however, among the causes should be placed an exceedingly simple and prosaic fact which seems to have escaped notice. I refer to the displacement of the dinner hour, and the ceremony now surrounding that meal.

Forty years ago dinner was still a simple affair, taken at hours varying from three to five o'clock, and uniting few but the members of a family, holidays and fetes being the rare occasions when guests were asked. There was probably not a hotel in this country at that time where a dinner was served later than three o'clock, and Delmonico's, newly installed in Mr.

Moses Grinnell's house, corner of Fourteenth Street and Fifth Avenue, was the only establishment of its kind in America, and the one restaurant in New York where ladies could be taken to dine. In those tranquil days when dinner parties were few and dances a rarity, theatre-going was the one ripple on the quiet stream of home life. Wallack's, at the corner of Thirteenth Street and Broadway, Booth's in Twenty-third Street, and Fechter's in Fourteenth Street were the homes of good comedy and high-class tragedy.

Along about 1870 the more aristocratically-minded New Yorkers took to dining at six or six-thirty o'clock; since then each decade has seen the dinner recede further into the night, until it is a common occurrence now to sit down to that repast at eight or even nine o'clock. Not only has the hour changed, but the meal itself has undergone a radical transformation, in keeping with the general increase of luxurious living, becoming a serious although hurried function. In consequence, to go to the theatre and be present at the rising of the curtain means, for the majority possessing sufficient means to go often to the play and culture enough to be discriminating, the disarrangement of the entire machinery of a household as well as the habits of its inmates.

In addition to this, dozens of sumptuous establishments have sprung up where the pleasure of eating is supplemented by allurements to the eye and ear. Fine orchestras play nightly, the air is laden with the perfume of flowers, a scenic perspective of palm garden and marble corridor flatters the senses. The temptation, to a man wearied by a day of business or sport, to abandon the idea of going to a theatre, and linger instead over his cigar amid these attractive surroundings, is almost irresistible.

If, however, tempted by some success, he hurries his guests away from their meal, they are in no condition to appreciate a serious performance. The pressure has been too high all day for the overworked man and his enervee wife to desire any but the lightest tomfoolery in an entertainment. People engaged in the lethargic process of digestion are not good critics of either elevated poetry or delicate interpretation, and in consequence crave amusement rather than a mental stimulant.

Managers were quick to perceive that their productions were no longer taken seriously, and that it was a waste of time and money to offer high-class entertainments to audiences whom any nonsense would attract. When a play like The Swell Miss Fitzwell will pack a New York house for months, and then float a company on the high tide of success across the continent, it would be folly to produce anything better. New York influences the taste of the country; it is in New York really that the standard has been lowered.

In answer to these remarks, the question will doubtless be raised, "Are not the influences which it is asserted are killing the drama in America at work in England or on the Continent, where people also dine late and well?"

Yes, and no! People abroad dine as well, undoubtedly; as elaborately? Certainly not! With the exception of the English (and even among them dinner-giving has never become so universal as with us), no other people entertain for the pleasure of hospitality. On the Continent, a dinner-party is always an "axe-grinding" function. A family who asked people to dine without having a distinct end in view for such an outlay would be looked upon by their friends and relatives as little short of lunatics. Diplomatists are allowed certain sums by their governments for entertaining, and are formally dined in return by their guests. A great French lady who is asked to dine out twice a week considers herself fortunate; a New York woman of equal position hardly dines at home from December 1 to April 15, unless she is receiving friends at her own table.

Parisian ladies rarely go to restaurants. In London there are not more than three or four places where ladies can be taken to dine, while in this city there are hundreds; our people have caught the habit of dining away from home, a custom singularly in keeping with the American temperament; for, although it costs more, it is less trouble!

The reason why foreigners do not entertain at dinner is because they have found other and more satisfactory ways of spending their money. This leaves people abroad with a number of evenings on their hands, unoccupied hours that are generally passed at the theatre. Only the other day a diplomatist said to me, "I am surprised to see how small a place the theatre occupies in your thoughts and conversation. With us it is the pivot around which life revolves."

From one cause or another, not only the wealthy, but the thoughtful and cultivated among us, go less each year to the theatre. The abstinence of this class is the most significant, for well-read, refined, fastidious citizens are the pride of a community, and their influence for good is far-reaching. Of this elite New York has more than its share, but you will not meet them at the play, unless Duse or Jefferson, Bernhardt or Coquelin is performing. The best only tempts such minds. It was by the encouragement of this class that Booth was enabled to give Hamlet one hundred consecutive evenings, and Fechter was induced to linger here and build a theatre.

In comparison with the verdicts of such people, the opinions of fashionable sets are of little importance. The latter long ago gave up going to the play in New York, except during two short seasons, one in the autumn, "before things get going," and again in the spring, after the season is over, before they flit abroad or to the country. During these periods "smart" people generally attend in bands called "theatre parties," an infliction unknown outside of this country, an arrangement above all others calculated to bring the stage into contempt, as such parties seldom arrive before the middle of the second act, take ten minutes to get seated, and then chat gayly among themselves for the rest of the evening.

The theatre, having ceased to form an integral part of our social life, has come to be the pastime of people with nothing better to do, - the floating population of our hotels, the shop-girl and her young man enjoying an evening out. The plays produced by the gentlemen who, I am told, control the stage in this country for the moment, are adapted to the requirements of an audience that, having no particular standard from which to judge the literary merits of a play, the training, accent, or talent of the actors, are perfectly contented so long as they are amused. To get a laugh, at any price, has become the ambition of most actors and the dream of managers.

A young actress in a company that played an American translation of Mme. Sans Gene all over this continent asked me recently what I thought of their performance. I said I thought it "a burlesque of the original!" "If you thought it a burlesque here in town," she answered, "it's well you didn't see us on the road. There was no monkey trick we would not play to raise a laugh."

If one of my readers doubts the assertion that the better classes have ceased to attend our theatres, except on rare occasions, let him inquire about, among the men and women whose opinions he values and respects, how many of last winter's plays they considered intellectual treats, or what piece tempted them to leave their cosy dinner-tables a second time. It is surprising to find the number who will answer in reply to a question about the merits of a play en vogue, "I have not seen it. In fact I rarely go to a theatre unless I am in London or on the Continent!"

Little by little we have taken to turning in a vicious and ever-narrowing circle. The poorer the plays, the less clever people will make the effort necessary to see them, and the less such elite attend, the poorer the plays will become.

That this state of affairs is going to last, however, I do not believe. The darkest hour is ever the last before the dawn. As it would he difficult for the performances in most of our theatres to fall any lower in the scale of frivolity or inanity, we may hope for a reaction that will be deep and far-reaching. At present we are like people dying of starvation because they do not know how to combine the flour and water and yeast before them into wholesome bread. The materials for a brilliant and distinctly national stage undoubtedly exist in this country. We have men and women who would soon develop into great actors if they received any encouragement to devote themselves to a higher class of work, and certainly our great city does not possess fewer appreciative people than it did twenty years ago.

The great dinner-giving mania will eat itself out; and managers, feeling once more that they can count on discriminating audiences, will no longer dare to give garbled versions of French farces or feeble dramas as compiled from English novels, but, turning to our own poets and writers, will ask them to contribute towards the formation of an American stage literature.

When, finally, one of our poets gives us a lyric drama like Cyrano de Bergerac, the attractions of the dinner-table will no longer be strong enough to keep clever people away from the theatre, and the following conversation, which sums up the present situation, will become impossible.

Banker (to Crushed Tragedian). - No, I haven't seen you act. I have not been inside a theatre for two years!

C.T. - It's five years since I've been inside a bank!

CHAPTER 31

THE MODERN ASPASIA

Most of the historic cities of Europe have a distinct local color, a temperament, if one may be allowed the expression, of their own. The austere calm of Bruges or Ghent, the sensuous beauty of Naples, attract different natures. Florence has passionate devotees, who are insensible to the artistic grace of Venice or the stately quiet of Versailles. In Cairo one experiences an exquisite bien etre, a mindless, ambitionless contentment which, without being languor, soothes the nerves and tempts to indolent lotus-eating. Like a great hive, Rome depends on the memories that circle around her, storing, like bees, the centuries with their honey. Each of these cities must therefore leave many people unmoved, who after a passing visit, wander away, wondering at the enthusiasm of the worshippers.

Paris alone seems to possess the charm that bewitches all conditions, all ages, all degrees. To hold the frivolous-minded she paints her face and dances, leading them a round of folly, exhaustive alike to health and purse. For the student she assumes another mien, smiling encouragement, and urging him upward towards the highest standards, while posing as his model. She takes the dreaming lover of the past gently by the hand, and leading him into quiet streets and squares where she has stored away a wealth of hidden treasure, enslaves him as completely as her more sensual admirers.

Paris is no less adored by the vacant-minded, to whom neither art nor pleasure nor study appeal. Her caprices in fashion are received by the wives and daughters of the universe as laws, and obeyed with an unwavering faith, a mute obedience that few religions have commanded. Women who yawn through Italy and the East have, when one meets them in the French capital, the intense manner, the air of separation from things mundane, that is observable in pilgrims approaching the shrine of their deity. Mohammedans at Mecca must have some such look. In Paris women find themselves in the presence of those high priests whom they have long worshipped from a distance. It is useless to mention other subjects to the devotee, for they will not fix her attention. Her thoughts are with her heart, and that is far away.

When visiting other cities one feels that they are like honest married women, living quiet family lives, surrounded by their children. The French Aspasia, on the contrary, has never been true to any vow, but has, at the dictate of her passions, changed from royal and imperial to republican lovers, and back again, ruled by no laws but her caprices, and discarding each favorite in turn with insults when she has wearied of him. Yet sovereigns are her slaves, and leave their lands to linger in her presence; and rich strangers from the four corners of the earth come to throw their fortunes at her feet and bask a moment in her smiles.

Like her classic prototype, Paris is also the companion of the philosophers and leads the arts in her train. Her palaces are the meeting-places of the poets, the sculptors, the dramatists, and the painters, who are never weary of celebrating her perfections, nor of working for her adornment and amusement.

Those who live in the circle of her influence are caught up in a whirlwind of artistic production, and consume their brains and bodies in the vain hope of pleasing their idol and attracting her attention. To be loved by Paris is an ordeal that few natures can stand, for she wrings the lifeblood from her devotees and then casts them aside into oblivion. Paris, said one of her greatest writers, "aime a briser ses idoles!" As Ulysses and his companions fell, in other days, a prey to the allurements of Circe, so our powerful young nation has fallen more than any other under the influence of the French siren, and brings her a yearly tribute of gold which she receives with avidity, although in her heart there is little fondness for the giver.

Americans who were in Paris two years ago had an excellent opportunity of judging the sincerity of Parisian affection, and of sounding the depth and unselfishness of the love that this fickle city gives us in return for our homage. Not for one moment did she hesitate, but threw the whole weight of her influence and wit into the scale for Spain. If there is not at this moment a European alliance against America it is not from any lack of effort on her part towards that end.

The stand taken by la villa lumiere in that crisis caused many naive Americans, who believed that their weakness for the French capital was returned, a painful surprise. They imagined in the simplicity of their innocent hearts that she loved them for themselves, and have awakened, like other rich lovers, to the humiliating knowledge that a penniless neighbor was receiving the caresses that Croesus paid for. Not only did the entire Parisian press teem at that moment with covert insults directed towards us, but in society, at the clubs and tables of the aristocracy, it was impossible for an American to appear with self-respect, so persistently were our actions and our reasons for undertaking that war misunderstood and misrepresented. In the conversation of the salons and in the daily papers it was assumed that the Spanish were a race of noble patriots, fighting in the defence of a loved and loyal colony, while we were a horde of blatant cowards, who had long fermented a revolution in Cuba in order to appropriate that coveted island.

When the Spanish authorities allowed an American ship (surprised in one of her ports by the declaration of war) to depart unharmed, the fact was magnified into an act of almost ideal generosity; on the other hand, when we decided not to permit privateering, that announcement was received with derisive laughter as a pretentious pose to cover hidden interests. There is reason to believe, however, that this feeling in favor of Spain goes little further than the press and the aristocratic circles so dear to the American "climber"; the real heart of the French nation is as true to us as when a century ago she spent blood and treasure in our cause. It is the inconstant capital alone that, false to her role of liberator, has sided with the tyrant.

Yet when I wander through her shady parks or lean over her monumental quays, drinking in the beauty of the first spring days, intoxicated by the perfume of the flowers that the night showers have kissed into bloom; or linger of an evening over my coffee, with the brilliant life of the boulevards passing like a carnival procession before my eyes; when I sit in her theatres, enthralled by the genius of her actors and playwrights, or stand bewildered before the ten thousand paintings and statues of the Salon, I feel inclined, like a betrayed lover, to pardon my faithless mistress: she is too lovely to remain long angry with her. You realize she is false and will betray you again, laughing at you, insulting your weakness; but when she smiles all faults are forgotten; the ardor of her kisses blinds you to her inconstancy; she pours out a draught that no other hands can brew, and clasps you in arms so fair that life outside those fragile barriers seems stale and unprofitable.

Eliot Gregory

CHAPTER 32

A NATION IN A HURRY

In early days of steam navigation on the Mississippi, the river captains, it is said, had the playful habit, when pressed for time or enjoying a "spurt" with a rival, of running their engines with a darky seated on the safety-valve.

One's first home impression after a season of lazy Continental travelling and visiting in somnolent English country houses, is that an emblematical Ethiopian should be quartered on our national arms.

Zola tells us in Nouvelle Campagne that his vivid impressions are all received during the first twenty-four hours in a new surrounding, - the mind, like a photographic film, quickly losing its sensibility.

This fleeting receptiveness makes returning Americans painfully conscious of nerves in the home atmosphere, and the headlong pace at which our compatriots are living.

The habit of laying such faults to the climate is but a poor excuse. Our grandparents and their parents lived peaceful lives beneath these same skies, undisturbed by the morbid influences that are supposed to key us to such a painful concert pitch.

There was an Indian summer languor in the air as we steamed up the bay last October, that apparently invited repose; yet no sooner had we set foot on our native dock, and taken one good whiff of home air, than all our acquired calm disappeared. People who ten days before would have sat (at a journey's end) contentedly in a waiting-room, while their luggage was being sorted by leisurely officials, now hustle nervously about, nagging the custom-house officers and egging on the porters, as though the saving of the next half hour were the prime object of existence.

Considering how extravagant we Americans are in other ways it seems curious that we should be so economical of time! It was useless to struggle against the current, however, or to attempt to hold one's self back. Before ten minutes on shore had passed, the old, familiar, unpleasant sensation of being in a hurry took possession of me! It was irresistible and all-pervading; from the movements of the crowds in the streets to the whistle of the harbor tugs, everything breathed of haste. The very dogs had apparently no time to loiter, but scurried about as though late for their engagements.

The transit from dock to hotel was like a visit to a new circle in the Inferno, where trains rumble eternally overhead, and cable cars glide and block around a pale-faced throng of the damned, who are forced, in expiation of their sins, to hasten forever toward an unreachable goal.

A curious curse has fallen upon our people; an "influence" is at work which forces us to attempt in an hour just twice as much as can be accomplished in sixty minutes. "Do as well as you can," whispers the "influence," "but do it quickly!" That motto might be engraved upon the fronts of our homes and business buildings.

It is on account of this new standard that rapidity in a transaction on the Street is appreciated more than correctness of detail. A broker to-day will take more credit for having received and executed an order for Chicago and returned an answer within six minutes, than for any amount of careful work. The order may have been ill executed and the details mixed, but there will have been celerity of execution to boast of

The young man who expects to succeed in business to-day must be a "hustler," have a snap-shot style in conversation, patronize rapid transit vehicles, understand shorthand, and eat at "breathless breakfasts."

Being taken recently to one of these establishments for "quick lunch," as I believe the correct phrase is, to eat buckwheat cakes (and very good they were), I had an opportunity of studying the ways of the modern time-saving young man.

It is his habit upon entering to dash for the bill-of-fare, and give an order (if he is adroit enough to catch one of the maids on the fly) before removing either coat or hat. At least fifteen seconds may be economized in this way. Once seated, the luncher falls to on anything at hand; bread, cold slaw, crackers, or catsup. When the dish ordered arrives, he gets his fork into it as it appears over his shoulder, and has cleaned the plate before the sauce makes its appearance, so that is eaten by itself or with bread.

Cups of coffee or tea go down in two swallows. Little piles of cakes are cut in quarters and disappear in four mouthfuls, much after the fashion of children down the ogre's throat in the mechanical toy, mastication being either a lost art or considered a foolish waste of energy.

A really accomplished luncher can assimilate his last quarter of cakes, wiggle into his coat, and pay his check at the desk at the same moment. The next, he is down the block in pursuit of a receding trolley.

To any one fresh from the Continent, where the entire machinery of trade comes to a standstill from eleven to one o'clock, that dejeuner may be taken in somnolent tranquillity, the nervous tension pervading a restaurant here is prodigious, and what is worse - catching! During recent visits to the business centres of our city, I find that the idea of eating is repugnant. It seems to be wrong to waste time on anything so unproductive. Last week a friend offered me a "luncheon tablet" from a box on his desk. "It's as good as a meal," he said, "and so much more expeditious!"

The proprietor of one down-town restaurant has the stock quotations exhibited on a black-board at the end of his room; in this way his patrons can keep in touch with the "Street" as they hurriedly stoke up.

A parlor car, toward a journey's end, is another excellent place to observe our native ways. Coming from Washington the other day my fellow-passengers began to show signs of restlessness near Newark. Books and papers were thrown aside; a general "uprising, unveiling" followed, accompanied by our objectionable custom of having our clothes brushed in each other's faces. By the time Jersey City appeared on the horizon, every man, woman, and child in that car was jammed, baggage in hand, into the stuffy little passage which precedes the entrance, swaying and staggering about while the train backed and delayed.

The explanation of this is quite simple. The "influence" was at work, preventing those people from acting like other civilized mortals, and remaining seated until their train had come to a standstill.

Being fresh from the "other side," and retaining some of my acquired calm, I sat in my chair! The surprise on the faces of the other passengers warned me, however, that it would not be safe to carry this pose too far. The porter, puzzled by the unaccustomed sight, touched me kindly on the shoulder, and asked if I "felt sick"! So now, to avoid all affectation of superiority, I struggled into my great-coat, regardless of eighty degrees temperature in the car, and meekly joined the standing army of martyrs, to hurry, scampering with them from the still-moving car to the boat, and on to the trolley before the craft had been moored to its landing pier.

In Paris, on taking an omnibus, you are given a number and the right to the first vacant seat. When the places in a "bus" are all occupied it receives no further occupants. Imagine a traction line attempting such a reform here! There would be a riot, and the conductors hanged to the nearest trolley-poles in an hour!

To prevent a citizen from crowding into an over-full vehicle, and stamping on its occupants in the process, would be to infringe one of his dearest privileges, not to mention his chance of riding free.

A small boy of my acquaintance tells me he rarely

finds it necessary to pay in a New York car. The conductors are too hurried and too preoccupied pocketing their share of the receipts to keep count. "When he passes, I just look blank!" remarked the ingenious youth.

Of all the individuals, however, in the community, our idle class suffer the most acutely from lack of time, though, like Charles Lamb's gentleman, they have all there is.

From the moment a man of leisure, or his wife, wakens in the morning until they drop into a fitful slumber at night, their day is an agitated chase. No matter where or when you meet them, they are always on the wing.

"Am I late again?" gasped a thin little woman to me the other evening, as she hurried into the drawing-room, where she had kept her guests and dinner waiting. "I've been so driven all day, I'm a wreck!" A glance at her hatchet-faced husband revealed the fact that he, too, was chasing after a stray half-hour lost somewhere in his youth. His color and most of his hair had gone in its pursuit, while his hands had acquired a twitch, as though urging on a tired steed.

Go and ask that lady for a cup of tea at twilight; ten to one she will receive you with her hat on, explaining that she has not had time to take it off since breakfast. If she writes to you, her notes are signed, "In great haste," or "In a tearing hurry." She is out of her house by half-past eight on most mornings, yet when calling she sits on the edge of her chair, and assures you that she has not a moment to stay, "has only run in," etc.

Just what drives her so hard is a mystery, for beyond a

vague charity meeting or two and some calls, she accomplishes little. Although wealthy and childless, with no cares and few worries, she succumbs to nervous prostration every two or three years, "from overwork."

Listen to a compatriot's account of his European trip! He will certainly tell you how short the ocean crossing was, giving hours and minutes with zest, as though he had got ahead of Father Time in a transaction. Then follows a list of the many countries seen during his tour.

I know a lady lying ill to-day because she would hurry herself and her children, in six weeks last summer, through a Continental tour that should have occupied three months. She had no particular reason for hurrying; indeed, she got ahead of her schedule, and had to wait in Paris for the steamer; a detail, however, that in no way diminished madame's pleasure in having done so much during her holiday. This same lady deplores lack of leisure hours, yet if she finds by her engagement book that there is a free week ahead, she will run to Washington or Lakewood, "for a change," or organize a party to Florida.

To realize how our upper ten scramble through existence, one must also contrast their fidgety way of feeding with the bovine calm in which a German absorbs his nourishment and the hours Italians can pass over their meals; an American dinner party affords us the opportunity.

There is an impression that the fashion for quickly served dinners came to us from England. If this is true (which I doubt; it fits too nicely with our temperament to have been imported), we owe H.R.H. a debt of gratitude, for nothing is so tiresome as too many courses needlessly prolonged.

Like all converts, however, we are too zealous. From oysters to fruit, dinners now are a breathless steeple-chase, during which we take our viand hedges and champagne ditches at a dead run, with conversation pushed at much the same speed. To be silent would be to imply that one was not having a good time, so we rattle and gobble on toward the finger-bowl winning-post, only to find that rest is not there!

As the hostess pilots the ladies away to the drawing-room, she whispers to her spouse, "You won't smoke long, will you?" So we are mulcted in the enjoyment of even that last resource of weary humanity, the cigar, and are hustled away from that and our coffee, only to find that our appearance is a signal for a general move.

One of the older ladies rises; the next moment the whole circle, like a flock of frightened birds, are up and off, crowding each other in the hallway, calling for their carriages, and confusing the unfortunate servants, who are trying to help them into their cloaks and overshoes.

Bearing in mind that the guests come as late as they dare, without being absolutely uncivil, that dinners are served as rapidly as is physically possible, and that the circle breaks up as soon as the meal ends, one asks one's self in wonder why, if a dinner party is such a bore that it has to be scrambled through, coute que coute, we continue to dine out?

It is within the bounds of possibility that people may

have reasons for hurrying through their days, and that dining out a la longue becomes a weariness.

The one place, however, where you might expect to find people reposeful and calm is at the theatre. The labor of the day is then over; they have assembled for an hour or two of relaxation and amusement. Yet it is at the play that our restlessness is most apparent. Watch an audience (which, be it remarked in passing, has arrived late) during the last ten minutes of a performance. No sooner do they discover that the end is drawing near than people begin to struggle into their wraps. By the time the players have lined up before the footlights the house is full of disappearing backs.

Past, indeed, are the unruffled days when a heroine was expected (after the action of a play had ended) to deliver the closing envoi dear to the writers of Queen Anne's day. Thackeray writes:-

> *The play is done! The curtain drops,*
> *Slow falling to the prompter's bell!*
> *A moment yet the actor stops,*
> *And looks around, to say farewell!*

A comedian who attempted any such abuse of the situation to-day would find himself addressing empty benches. Before he had finished the first line of his epilogue, most of his public would be housed in the rapid transit cars. No talent, no novelty holds our audiences to the end of a performance.

On the opening night of the opera season this winter, one third of the "boxes" and orchestra stalls were vacant before Romeo (who, being a foreigner, was taking his time) had expired.

One overworked matron of my acquaintance has perfected an ingenious and time-saving combination. By signalling from a window near her opera box to a footman below, she is able to get her carriage at least two minutes sooner than her neighbors.

During the last act of an opera like Tann-hauser or Faust, in which the inconsiderate composer has placed a musical gem at the end, this lady is worth watching. After getting into her wraps and overshoes she stands, hand on the door, at the back of her box, listening to the singers; at a certain moment she hurries to the window, makes her signal, scurries back, hears Calve pour her soul out in Anges purs, anges radieux, yet manages to get down the stairs and into her carriage before the curtain has fallen.

We deplore the prevailing habit of "slouch"; yet if you think of it, this universal hurry is the cause of it. Our cities are left unsightly, because we cannot spare time to beautify them. Nervous diseases are distressingly prevalent; still we hurry! hurry!! hurry!!! until, as a diplomatist recently remarked to me, the whole nation seemed to him to be but five minutes ahead of an apoplectic fit.

The curious part of the matter is that after several weeks at home, much that was strange at first becomes quite natural to the traveller, who finds himself thinking with pity of benighted foreigners and their humdrum ways, and would resent any attempts at reform.

What, for instance, would replace for enterprising souls the joy of taking their matutinal car at a flying leap, or the rapture of being first out of a theatre? What does part of a last act or the "star song" matter in comparison with five minutes of valuable time to the good? Like the river captains, we propose to run under full head of steam and get there, or b - explode!

CHAPTER 33

THE SPIRIT OF HISTORY

Buildings become tombs when the race that constructed them has disappeared. Libraries and manuscripts are catacombs where most of us might wander in the dark forever, finding no issue. To know dead generations and their environments through these channels, to feel a love so strong that it calls the past forth from its winding-sheet, and gives it life again, as Christ did Lazarus, is the privilege only of great historians.

France is honoring the memory of such a man at this moment; one who for forty years sought the vital spark of his country's existence, striving to resuscitate what he called "the great soul of history," as it developed through successive acts of the vast drama. This employment of his genius is Michelet's title to fame.

In a sombre structure, the tall windows of which look across the Luxembourg trees to the Pantheon, where her husband's bust has recently been placed, a widow preserves with religious care the souvenirs of this great historian. Nothing that can recall either his life or his labor is changed.

Madame Michelet's life is in strange contrast with the

ways of the modern spouse who, under pretext of grief, discards and displaces every reminder of the dead. In our day, when the great art is to forget, an existence consecrated to a memory is so rare that the world might be the better for knowing that a woman lives who, young and beautiful, was happy in the society of an old man, whose genius she appreciated and cherished, who loves him dead as she loved him living. By her care the apartment remains as it stood when he left it, to die at Hyeres, - the furniture, the paintings, the writing-table. No stranger has sat in his chair, no acquaintance has drunk from his cup. This woman, who was a perfect wife and now fills one's ideal of what a widow's life should be, has constituted herself the vigilant guardian of her husband's memory. She loves to talk of the illustrious dead, and tell how he was fond of saying that Virgil and Vico were his parents. Any one who reads the Georgicsor The Bird will see the truth of this, for he loved all created things, his ardent spiritism perceiving that the essence which moved the ocean's tides was the same that sang in the robin at the window during his last illness, which he called his "little captive soul."

The author of La Bible de l'Humanite had to a supreme degree the love of country, and possessed the power of reincarnating with each succeeding cycle of its history. So luminous was his mind, so profound and far-reaching his sympathy, that he understood the obscure workings of the mediaeval mind as clearly as he appreciated Mirabeau's transcendent genius. He believed that humanity, like Prometheus, was self-made; that nations modelled their own destiny during the actions and reactions of history, as each one of us acquires a personality through the struggles and temptations of existence, by the evolving power every soul carries within itself.

Michelet taught that each nation was the hero of its own drama; that great men have not been different from the rest of their race - on the contrary, being the condensation of an epoch, that, no matter what the apparent eccentricities of a leader may have been, he was the expression of a people's spirit. This discovery that a race is transformed by its action upon itself and upon the elements it absorbs from without, wipes away at a stroke the popular belief in "predestined races" or providential "great men" appearing at crucial moments and riding victorious across the world.

An historian, if what he writes is to have any value, must know the people, the one great historical factor. Radicalism in history is the beginning of truth. Guided by this light of his own, Michelet discovered a fresh factor heretofore unnoticed, that vast fermentation which in France transforms all foreign elements into an integral part of the country's being. After studying his own land through the thirteen centuries of her growth, from the chart of Childebert to the will of Louis XVI., Michelet declared that while England is a composite empire and Germany a region, France is a personality. In consequence he regarded the history of his country as a long dramatic poem. Here we reach the inner thought of the historian, the secret impulse that guided his majestic pen.

The veritable hero of his splendid Iliad is at first ignorant and obscure, seeking passionately like OEdipus to know himself. The interest of the piece is absorbing. We can follow the gradual development of his nature as it becomes more attractive and sympathetic with each advancing age, until, through the hundred acts of the tragedy, he achieves a soul. For Michelet to write the history of his country was to describe the long evolution of a hero. He was fond of telling his friends that during the Revolution of July, while he was making his translation of Vico, this great fact was revealed to him in the blazing vision of a people in revolt. At that moment the young and unknown author resolved to devote his life, his talents, his gift of clairvoyance, the magic of his inimitable style and creative genius, to fixing on paper the features seen in his vision.

Conceived and executed in this spirit, his history could be but a stupendous epic, and proves once again the truth of Aristotle's assertion that there is often greater truth in poetry than in prose.

Seeking in the remote past for the origin of his hero, Michelet pauses first before the Cathedral. The poem begins like some mediaeval tale. The first years of his youthful country are devoted to a mystic religion. Under his ardent hands vast naves rise and belfries touch the clouds. It is but a sad and cramped development, however; statutes restrain his young ardor and chill his blood. It is not until the boy is behind the plough in the fields and sunlight that his real life begins - a poor, brutish existence, if you will, but still life. The "Jacques," half man and half beast, of the Middle Ages is the result of a thousand years of suffering.

A woman's voice calls this brute to arms. An enemy is overrunning the land. Joan the virgin - "my Joan," Michelet calls her - whose heart bleeds when blood is shed, frees her country. A shadow, however, soon obscures this gracious vision from Jacques's eyes. The vast monarchical incubus rises between the people and their ideal. Our historian turns in disgust from the later French kings. He has neither time nor heart to write their history, so passes quickly from Louis XI. to the great climax of his drama - the Revolution. There we find his hero, emerging at last from tyranny and oppression. Freedom and happiness are before him. Alas! his eyes, accustomed to the dim light of dungeons, are dazzled by the sun of liberty; he strikes friend and foe alike.

In the solitary galleries of the "Archives" Michelet communes with the great spirits of that day, Desaix, Marceau, Kleber, - elder sons of the Republic, who whisper many secrets to their pupil as he turns over faded pages tied with tri-colored ribbons, where the cities of France have written their affection for liberty, love-letters from Jacques to his mistress. Michelet is happy. His long labor is drawing to an end. The great epic which he has followed as it developed through the centuries is complete. His hero stands hand in hand before the altar with the spouse of his choice, for whose smile he has toiled and struggled. The poet-historian sees again in the Fete de la Federation the radiant face of his vision, the true face of France, La Dulce.

Through all the lyricism of this master's work one feels that he has "lived" history as he wrote it, following his subject from its obscure genesis to a radiant apotheosis. The faithful companion of Michelet's age has borne witness to this power which he possessed of projecting himself into another age and living with his subject. She repeats to those who know her how he trembled in passion and burned with patriotic emotion in transcribing the crucial pages of his country's history, rejoicing in her successes and depressed by her faults, like the classic historian who refused with horror to tell the story of his compatriots' defeat at Cannae, saying, "I could not survive the recital."

"Do you remember," a friend once asked Madame Michelet, "how, when your husband was writing his chapters on the Reign of Terror, he ended by falling ill?"

"Ah, yes!" she replied. "That was the week he executed Danton. We were living in the country near Nantes. The ground was covered with snow. I can see him now, hurrying to and fro under the bare trees, gesticulating and crying as he walked, 'How can I judge them, those great men? How can I judge them?' It was in this way that he threw his 'thousand souls' into the past and lived in sympathy with all men, an apostle of universal love. After one of these fecund hours he would drop into his chair and murmur, 'I am crushed by this work. I have been writing with my blood!'"

Alas, his aged eyes were destined to read sadder pages than he had ever written, to see years as tragic as the "Terror." He lived to hear the recital of (having refused to witness) his country's humiliation, and fell one April morning, in his retirement near Pisa, unconscious under the double shock of invasion and civil war. Though he recovered later, his horizon remained dark. The patriot suffered to see party spirit and warring factions rending the nation he had so often called the pilot of humanity's bark, which seemed now to be going straight on the rocks. "Finis Galliae," murmured the historian, who to the end lived and died with his native land.

Thousands yearly mount the broad steps of the Pantheon to lay their wreaths upon his tomb, and thousands more in every Gallic schoolroom are daily learning, in the pages of his history, to love France la Dulce.

Choose from Thousands of 1stWorldLibrary Classics By

Adolphus WilliamWard	Clemence Housman	Gabrielle E. Jackson
Aesop	Confucius	Garrett P. Serviss
Agatha Christie	Cornelis DeWitt Wilcox	Gaston Leroux
Alexander Aaronsohn	Cyril Burleigh	George Ade
Alexander Kielland	D. H. Lawrence	Geroge Bernard Shaw
Alexandre Dumas	Daniel Defoe	George Ebers
Alfred Gatty	David Garnett	George Eliot
Alfred Ollivant	Don Carlos Janes	George MacDonald
Alice Duer Miller	Donald Keyhole	George Orwell
Alice Turner Curtis	Dorothy Kilner	George Tucker
Alice Dunbar	Dougan Clark	George W. Cable
Ambrose Bierce	E. Nesbit	George Wharton James
Amelia E. Barr	E.P.Roe	Gertrude Atherton
Andrew Lang	E. Phillips Oppenheim	Grace E. King
Andrew McFarland Davis	Edgar Allan Poe	Grant Allen
Anna Sewell	Edgar Rice Burroughs	Guillermo A. Sherwell
Annie Besant	Edith Wharton	Gulielma Zollinger
Annie Hamilton Donnell	Edward J. O'Biren	Gustav Flaubert
Annie Payson Call	John Cournos	H. A. Cody
Anton Chekhov	Edwin L. Arnold	H. B. Irving
Arnold Bennett	Eleanor Atkins	H. G. Wells
Arthur Conan Doyle	Elizabeth Cleghorn	H. H. Munro
Arthur Ransome	Gaskell	H. Irving Hancock
Atticus	Elizabeth Von Arnim	H. Rider Haggard
B. M. Bower	Ellem Key	H. W. C. Davis
Basil King	Emily Dickinson	Hamilton Wright Mable
Bayard Taylor	Erasmus W. Jones	Hans Christian Andersen
Ben Macomber	Ernie Howard Pie	Harold Avery
Booth Tarkington	Ethel Turner	Harold McGrath
Bram Stoker	Ethel Watts Mumford	Harriet Beecher Stowe
C. Collodi	Eugenie Foa	Harry Houidini
C. E. Orr	Eugene Wood	Helent Hunt Jackson
C. M. Ingleby	Evelyn Everett-Green	Helen Nicolay
Carolyn Wells	Everard Cotes	Hendy David Thoreau
Catherine Parr Traill	F. J. Cross	Henrik Ibsen
Charles A. Eastman	Federick Austin Ogg	Henry Adams
Charles Dickens	Ferdinand Ossendowski	Henry Ford
Charles Dudley Warner	Francis Bacon	Henry Frost
Charles Farrar Browne	Francis Darwin	Henry James
Charles Ives	Frances Hodgson Burnett	Henry Jones Ford
Charles Kingsley	Frank Gee Patchin	Henry Seton Merriman
Charles Lathrop Pack	Frank Harris	Henry Wadsworth
Charles Whibley	Frank Jewett Mather	Longfellow
Charles Willing Beale	Frank L. Packard	Henry W Longfellow
Charlotte M. Braeme	Frederick Trevor Hill	Herbert A. Giles
Charlotte M.Yonge	Frederick Winslow Taylor	Herbert N. Casson
Clair W. Hayes	Friedrich Kerst	Herman Hesse
Clarence Day Jr.	Friedrich Nietzsche	Homer
Clarence E. Mulford	Fyodor Dostoyevsky	Honore De Balzac

Horace Walpole
Horatio Alger, Jr.
Howard Pyle
Howard R. Garis
Hugh Lofting
Hugh Walpole
Humphry Ward
Ian Maclaren
Israel Abrahams
J.G.Austin
J. Henri Fabre
J. M. Barrie
J. Macdonald Oxley
J. S. Knowles
J. Storer Clouston
Jack London
Jacob Abbott
James Allen
James Lane Allen
James Andrews
James Baldwin
James DeMille
James Joyce
James Oliver Curwood
James Oppenheim
James Otis
Jane Austen
Jens Peter Jacobsen
Jerome K. Jerome
John Burroughs
John F. Kennedy
John Gay
John Glasworthy
John Habberton
John Joy Bell
John Milton
John Philip Sousa
Jonathan Swift
Joseph Carey
Joseph Conrad
Joseph Jacobs
Julian Hawthrone
Julies Vernes
Justin Huntly McCarthy
Kakuzo Okakura
Kenneth Grahame
Kate Langley Bosher
L. A. Abbot
L. T. Meade
L. Frank Baum
Laura Lee Hope

Laurence Housman
Leo Tolstoy
Leonid Andreyev
Lewis Carroll
Lilian Bell
Lloyd Osbourne
Louis Tracy
Louisa May Alcott
Lucy Fitch Perkins
Lucy Maud Montgomery
Lydia Miller Middleton
Lyndon Orr
M. H. Adams
Margaret E. Sangster
Margaret Vandercook
Maria Edgeworth
Maria Thompson Daviess
Mariano Azuela
Marion Polk Angellotti
Mark Overton
Mark Twain
Mary Austin
Mary Cole
Mary Rowlandson
Mary Wollstonecraft
Shelley
Max Beerbohm
Myra Kelly
Nathaniel Hawthrone
O. F. Walton
Oscar Wilde
Owen Johnson
P.G.Wodehouse
Paul and Mable Thorn
Paul G. Tomlinson
Paul Severing
Peter B. Kyne
Plato
R. Derby Holmes
R. L. Stevenson
Rabindranath Tagore
Rahul Alvares
Ralph Waldo Emmerson
Rene Descartes
Rex E. Beach
Richard Harding Davis
Richard Jefferies
Robert Barr
Robert Frost
Robert Gordon Anderson
Robert L. Drake

Robert Lansing
Robert Michael Ballantyne
Robert W. Chambers
Rosa Nouchette Carey
Ross Kay
Rudyard Kipling
Samuel B. Allison
Samuel Hopkins Adams
Sarah Bernhardt
Selma Lagerlof
Sherwood Anderson
Sigmund Freud
Standish O'Grady
Stanley Weyman
Stella Benson
Stephen Crane
Stewart Edward White
Stijn Streuvels
Swami Abhedananda
Swami Parmananda
T. S. Ackland
The Princess Der Ling
Thomas A. Janvier
Thomas A Kempis
Thomas Anderton
Thomas Bailey Aldrich
Thomas Bulfinch
Thomas De Quincey
Thomas H. Huxley
Thomas Hardy
Thomas More
Thornton W. Burgess
U. S. Grant
Valentine Williams
Victor Appleton
Virginia Woolf
Walter Scott
Washington Irving
Wilbur Lawton
Wilkie Collins
Willa Cather
Willard F. Baker
William Makepeace
Thackeray
William W. Walter
Winston Churchill
Yei Theodora Ozaki
Young E. Allison
Zane Grey